TORMENT

TORMENT

JUNE ZETTER

authorHOUSE®

AuthorHouse™ UK
1663 Liberty Drive
Bloomington, IN 47403 USA
www.authorhouse.co.uk
Phone: 0800.197.4150

Published by AuthorHouse 12/09/2014

ISBN: 978-1-4969-9771-5 (sc)
ISBN: 978-1-4969-9779-1 (e)

ANN WAS FOURTEEN years old and should have been in school today. Her mother had been very angry with her last night. "Straight home from school tomorrow" She'd shouted. "You are grounded for a week". That awful bloody school teacher had informed on her again. "She hasn't handed in any of her home work and refuses to do it". She'd said. All day they worked hard at lessons and were expected to do more on a night time, it just wasn't fair. Ann decided she was going to the park instead of school, she was fed up of being told what she could or couldn't do. A man was sitting on a park bench smiling at her, did she look funny? She looked in the opposite direction and found another bench to sit on; she didn't like strangers smiling at her. He was still smiling when she stood up to go. The man was saying something which she didn't quite hear. "Sorry" She said. "Were you speaking to me"? He laughed at her saying. "I don't mean to be rude and I apologise but you look as though I am about to eat you and I would rather eat this sandwich". He held out a sandwich to her, she hesitated for a second before taking it while he continued eating the other one. "They are only cheese with a little tomato; it was all the shop had I hope you like it". Ann was quite hungry as it was now mid day and she had left home at seven thirty in the morning. He offered her a drink, she took it taking a good swallow and started coughing. The man patted her back. "I think you drank too much at one go". He said, lifting up the bottle again to her lips. "Try drinking it more slowly". Ann opened her mouth for a sip. "It's making my throat hot". She said. He smiled at her. "That's ok". He replied. "There's a lot of ginger in it and it burns my throat too". He continued saying "You did take a good drink, you aught to have sipped it like you are doing now". He was such a nice man and she was pleased she had met him, much better than going to school. "Do you want another drink? This bottle is almost empty and you seem to be enjoying it". He was so kind, Ann thought as she picked up the bottle and drained it before handing it back. Now it was her turn to laugh and she didn't know why. As if by magic another full bottle appeared. "I am not thirsty" Ann said and I think its time to go before mom comes looking for me" She stood up and fell back down, the man caught her. "Your mother knows you are here?" He asked. "She will now because the teacher will have rung her from school and she will be looking for me". Ann knew she would be in trouble when her mother found her. "Have you ever played at Hide and Seek?" He asked. "Every bodies played that game" Ann answered. Did he think she was a little girl? "I meant hiding from your mother or teacher or whoever else is looking for you". She was trying to stand up again and started giggling. "Show me where we can hide and I will be quiet as a mouse" He put his arm around her waist saying "I have a car parked around the corner we could hide in there but we will have to keep our heads down or we will be seen". "I am not supposed to get into strangers cars" Ann said. "But you're not a stranger now, are you? I feel thirsty again can I have another drink?" "Not yet" He replied. "When we reach the car you can drink the bottle dry". He was finding it hard work keeping her on her feet and she was moving too slowly. "We have to hurry" He was becoming agitated they would be seen. "I could give you a fire mans lift and pretend you are being rescued, would you like that?" He smiled his lovely smile at her. "Yes please" She giggled and over his shoulder she went like a rag doll. How good it felt having her hanging there breathing, sighing and moving provocatively on his shoulder. She was enjoying this and he felt she was trying to show him just how much as she wriggled about on his back. The thought of taking and controlling her every move was thrilling him and it had to be soon. The car was parked in a quiet cull de sac and Ann had fallen asleep on his shoulder, the drink had worked. It was awkward getting her into the car as now she was a dead weight. He laid her onto the back seat accidently knocking her head on the door; he bent over to kiss her gently on the forehead before running his hands up and down her thighs and squeezing the inner parts. He stood up holding onto the car door shaking with anticipation. She was beautiful and so young and he wanted her now but he would have to take her far away from this place before his feelings could be fulfilled. It would be a while before she awoke and he knew she would be wanting and needing him too, he could feel the tremors in her burning limbs. Starting the car he moved out from the cull de sac and noticed a woman in the park who looked as though she was searching for something or someone, he wasn't stopping to find out which. Out on the motorway Ann started moving but lucky for him she was still drowsy and wanted a drink. He would pull out onto a bypass and give her some more it should keep her quiet until he reached his destination. Taking the first road off the motor way he found a place to pull over. It was fairly dark; if the moon hadn't been shining it would have been too dark to see as his car lights were turned off. Ann was asking for a drink again and he let her drink half of the bottle. All the time he kept watching as she moved around in the back seat, her thighs fully exposed. He stroked them and they were hot, his hand began to slide upwards. Suddenly she sat up taking off her jacket and asked "Where are we? He removed his hands quickly before answering. "We are hiding remember". He said as he tipped the bottle again. "Are you feeling too warm?" He asked. "Yes" Ann sighed and closed her eyes again. "Let me help you remove your woollen school jumper it's much too hot for you" What a kind man he was and she was having such a lovely dream. Her head hurting when she awoke, it was dark and smelt of animals, where was she? Ann was trying to remember what had happened but her head was spinning and aching and she couldn't think quickly enough. Feeling the call of nature she tried to get up as it had been a while since she had relieved herself. It was impossible her hands were tied and she was fastened onto the inside of what seemed to be an old stable. She could feel the rough straw beneath her. "How has this happened?" She asked herself. "Who could have tied me up?" She was still under the influence of the drink and the dope that he had mixed with it, so although worried she wasn't thinking rationally. A light shone from under a door and the sound of voices reached her. One voice she recognized it was her friend the man from the park, if he really was her friend? Another voice was deep and shouting loudly, someone else joined in and started shouting back, this voice belonged to a woman. Ann called out but they ignored her. She kicked at the wooden walls she was tied to and the sound echoed through the building. The light blinded her as the door opened and a huge frame yelled at her to be quiet. "I need the toilet" Ann cried. "I told you to shut up otherwise you'll get the back of my hand" He laughed saying. "That'll make you wee your pants" Then added. "Use the straw". "My hands are tied how can I do anything?" Even if she was afraid Ann had to ask for her hands to be untied. "I will untie her" The woman said. "You had better make sure you tie her up again". The voice of the man was harsh. "There's a lot of money coming from selling her. The big boys will be here in two hours and we can't take a chance with her absconding". The woman came over and bent down to untie her. "Don't do anything foolish" She said. "Or they will hurt you, it wouldn't be the first time they have disfigured a girl for not doing their bidding. So please behave yourself because I won't be able to save you." Ann's hands were sore and the pain from being unable to go to the toilet felt worse. "Where can I go?" She asked the woman. "Where he told you, go on the straw. There is no where else ". Ann didn't argue she used the straw, it was an immense relief. "Why are you keeping me here?" Ann asked the female. "Do you remember how you got here?" The woman enquired. "No" Ann answered. "You met a man in the park, didn't you?" The woman said. How did she know about the park did she know him? Ann was puzzled. The woman picked up the rope to tie her up again. "Just a few minutes first please" Ann begged. "My hands hurt so much". "Ok" She answered. "I'll give you a break for a little while as it can't be much fun sitting here in the dark on your own". She was making a joke of it. Ann realized she couldn't have any feelings to want to be part of hurting her. "You asked me if I remembered the man in the park and I do" Ann said. He was a kind handsome man. What happened to him was he captured too?" This time the woman couldn't stop laughing and the man on the other side of the door called for her to tie the bitch up and get back out. "Sorry dearie but I have to tie you up again". She was being apologetic. "I won't fasten them as tight as they were before, he shouldn't have bound you so tightly. You were doped and wouldn't have been able to run away. He really is a sadistic monster". She offered her a drink and Ann shook her head. "Its only water it can't hurt you" She sipped it and yes, it was water and she was grateful for it. "Who was it that tied me up so tightly?" Ann wanted to know. "How can all you girls be so innocent and naive" The woman answered her. "It was your friend from the park, he doped you and if we had arrived later you would have been in a more sorry state than you are now. He is not a man to be trusted with young females and gets his excitement from hurting them and prolonging their pain. You may not think you are lucky but believe me, you are" She tested the ropes making sure they were well tied and left Ann alone. She was cold and very frightened and the darkness made it worse, there were no windows only the door which led to the angry voices. A light shone under the door and she could see their feet pacing up and down. She wanted her mother and started to cry. She would be looking for her and she too would be crying. Why hadn't she gone to school like all her friends and what was going to happen to her, were they going to kill her? She lay on the straw and cried herself to sleep and was awakened by someone shaking her. "You have to take a bath as you stink". It was the woman again. "Don't try to escape or you will be hurt, they say you are worth your weight in gold so they are not going to lose you". The woman untied Ann and pulled her onto her feet. Ann's legs hurt with the sudden movement as she had been asleep for a while and pins and needles had started. "Hurry up" The woman said. "I have new clothes for you to wear, when we get this smell off of you and I shall be bleaching your hair, it will make you more interesting to your new owners". Ann grabbed hold of the stable door. "I am not coming". She shouted. "I want to go back home you can't keep me here a prisoner, you have kidnapped me and the police will find me. You are all wicked and I hate you". The woman slapped her face hard saying." Shut up you little idiot, if they hear you all will be lost and you will never see your mother or anyone else ever again. If they think you will cause trouble they will dispose of you. For them it's easy, a little trip down the road to the pig farm". Ann was sobbing, the woman had hurt her "What have pigs got to do with me?" She was puzzled. The woman told her she was better off not knowing and dragged her toward the bathroom. The hot water and suds felt good, she was clean again but that woman was going to make her into a blonde. Her hair was long and wavy and almost black so why did they have to change it. Her mother would be so angry with them. "Time you got yourself dried off" The woman called. "I want to get your hair done". Ann got out of the bath and pulled the large towel around her self, sitting down closer to the sink. The woman was mixing something in a jug and she was wearing rubber gloves. "I don't know a lot about this bleaching" She said. "But I am told that it may sting a little so keep your eyes closed and if it starts burning tell me so I will be able to weaken it down a bit". It was taking a long time and the smell of bleach was making Ann's eyes water. The men shouted out their orders to the woman a couple of times telling her to hurry up and give the bitch something to eat with some special sweet coffee to drink and to make sure that its extra sweet "Beauty can't be rushed" She had replied. "But if you two would like to do it, you are welcome". And the shouting ceased. Ann sat waiting for the bleach to work and she was given food plus a hot coffee, unknown to Ann a drug had been stirred into the coffee. She drank it all and asked for more which the woman was happy to give, mixing more of the drug with the sugar. What was going to happen after this? Ann didn't dare ask but she needed to know. They had said she was to be sold; it was a ridicules thing to say nobody sells people any more. History lessons had shown black slaves being sold to work the plantations for white people but that was in the olden days and slavery was no more. The woman interrupted her thoughts "Come here girl" She said. "Let's see how this bleach has worked". Ann's head was under the shower and she could see her long hair with the water dripping off it. Ann was shocked her hair wasn't blonde, it was white. "Looks good" The woman was pleased with the results and took out a hair dryer. "Is this how I have to keep it?" Ann asked the woman. "Yep, unless you want me to put stripes in it" She laughed and continued drying her hair. Ann was feeling relaxed but hadn't been able to see what the woman had done to her hair until she handed her a mirror. It was as if she was looking at someone older, it scared her and she was lost for words. The woman smiled at Ann's reflection saying "I knew this would be good they are going to be so surprised when they see you. Now we need to make your face pretty". She picked up a box of make up from the floor and said. "I have made up some famous faces for glossy magazines and television, I am an artist and can transform a face with brushes and you will be beautiful". "No, no" Ann pushed her away with tears in her eyes. "I don't want you to do any more". "Its fine by me" The woman answered shrugging her shoulders. "Might as well call it a day, you look good enough for what they want you for. Come on now move yourself". She threw clothes at her telling her to get them on." Put them on quickly or they'll be seeing you naked too soon and it's not very warm". Black underwear with sheer black stockings, a red tight fitting satin dress that zipped top to bottom at the front, with a wide gold belt. Three inch high heels, which Ann found hard keeping her balance on plus bright red sparkling ear rings which dangled around her face. This was no longer the fourteen year old school girl but one who looked and knew what life was all about. Ann was nervous and yet feeling excited for whatever came next, the drugs were working. The door opened and she was ushered into the other room. It was filled with the smoke of cigars, cigarettes and stank of sweat and drink. Four men were sitting there with their eyes peeled on her. The man from the park stood up and whispered into her ear. "Hello darling, you do look beautiful". His tongue began darting in and out of her ear turning and twisting inside it. Ann felt shivers running down her spine it was a strange feeling but she didn't answer him and turned her head away. The big man shouted at him. "You had your chance with her last night and lost it, now you're too late. We need her pretty not beaten black and blue. She's worth a great deal of money to us but not if you have your wicked ways with her". The other two men were looking impatient. One stood up and spoke with a foreign accent "We want to see her move around and see her smile it is important that she has good teeth. What is her breast size? He asked. "This we must know as the buyer insists on the measurements. Also her waist and hips and the proof that she is intact, a virgin". Ann couldn't believe what she was hearing they were going to sell her, it was all true. The second man who appeared to be foreign stood up; he didn't speak but took hold of her arm turning her around and around until she almost lost her balance. He caught hold of her as she wobbled and gripped her hard, one of his big hands started moving over her buttocks stroking and pinching. He began rubbing her belly almost lifting her off her feet with each upward rub. He was a large powerful man and she was afraid of trying to stop him. "Do you like me?" He asked. Ann didn't answer. "I said do you like me and do you like me doing this?" The man from the park looked at her saying "If you know what's good for you honey you had better answer yes and bloody smile like you mean it". Ann tried to smile and nodded her head. The man seemed happy as he watched her long blonde hair falling over her face with each nod and ran his fingers through the curls. He then proceeded to remove the gold belt from around her waist and threw it aside. He pulled her hands behind her holding them tightly in one hand and with the other he slowly unzipped the slinky dress to her waist. Her black bra was exposed; he could see her heaving breasts beneath and licked his lips. Without any warning he pushed his big hand under her dress pushing her legs apart and with his fat hairy fingers felt into the most intimate parts of her body. The watchers were all leaning in including the woman to look and see the other parts of her anatomy they hadn't seen before. Ann felt like a piece of meat they were all laughing drinking and smoking and the woman was using her camera. "Do you need any help there? A mans voice called. "I'm willing to give you a hand". The voice continued. Ann didn't know who asked that but it could have been her so called friend from the park. "Definitely not" Was the answer "Just watch and see how it's done" They continued watching and laughing at her. The man took his hand away and was smiling his approval. "Well done little one" He said, wiping his hands on a cloth. "You will go a long way and there are many tricks you shall learn on your travels especially how to make a man happy". Looking at Ann he began to smack his own backside with his hand, each slap was getting harder. He stopped hitting himself breathing heavily and lifted Ann under one arm carrying her over to a table and laying her face down. Lifting up her dress and pulling down her panties to her ankles he began to slap and knead her buttocks. He did it gently at first and Ann tried to hold her bottom tight. Her full round cheeks began taking on a pinkish hue which only invited him to continue. The others gathered closer not wanting to miss the show the big man wiped his lips onto his sleeve. The show was good but it was making him drool with excitement. The others kept touching her when they could, including the woman. He was now taking small bites and nibbles on her bottom and Ann was beginning to like the feeling it was giving her. A hand crept under her and was rubbing her breasts. Who's hand she didn't know but her nipples were hardening and she was wanting more. The biting stopped and the slapping began again, shaking the table she was lying on. Each slap getting harder until her buttocks were hot and stinging. Now it was hurting and she needed it to stop. He did stop, holding her there with her buttocks in the air. Taking a drink and a breather and wetting his hands to cool them he continued with faster slaps, which felt as if they were cutting into her skin. "Another ten minutes" He said breathing heavily. The slaps felt harder she was sure her bottom was on fire. He started the count down and the others joined in shouting and laughing. The final ten slaps were the toughest of all; he was using the gold belt. She could feel her bottom singeing, it was so very hot. She had never felt such pain and she was exhausted. "We will let you cool down now" He said. "A mans work is never done. Hard work can bring much enjoyment and I hope you enjoyed it too". He fell into a chair rubbing crème into his hands and grinning to himself. The man from the park leaned over his chair saying. "We watched you work with envy it is so good to see how an expert can manipulate his hands and fingers in such a rewarding way, we have much to learn." He hesitated before adding. "I for one would like to study your methods if only for a little while". "Not today" The man answered. "Maybe tomorrow we will see how we can introduce her to the leathers and twine. It may be a little too early but I am considered a good teacher as you have just seen. She has to learn quickly as her master requires a grade A. student and that is what I shall deliver to him". The beating was over and although Ann was hurting she felt excited, something had changed in her. Whoever it was they were still playing with her breasts someone else was cooling down her buttocks with ice. "Stop the bruising" they said. The man pulled Ann up roughly holding her against him, she felt wobbly and her feet hardly touched the ground. "I think we should have a little kiss" He said. "You have done really well, let me kiss you better". He took hold of Ann's face squeezing it with his hands until her lips stuck out. He then proceeded to suck her mouth into his own, she could hardly breathe. He seemed to know and let her up for air. She opened her mouth taking one gulp and his tongue thrust into the back of her throat. It felt like a snake was in her mouth shoving and pushing its way through. His rough hand tugged at her bra tearing it off and her breasts tumbled out. His mouth was on them nipping, biting, sucking deep, pummelling with his fingers and pulling the teats out as far as they would go and letting them go again. Once more his tongue searched deep inside her throat penetrating deeper than before. She felt herself sinking slowly onto the floor, or was she floating. He was still holding her and his tongue was still moving in and out of her mouth, she was exhausted. He saw this and lifted her up with his big hands under her crutch. He began squeezing his fingers tightly, as though he was trying to seal up her intimate parts and his nails were digging into her flesh. Grabbing her long hair he pulled her head back and began running his tongue up and down her torso. He let her go when her legs finally collapsed and crumbled under her. Picking up the gold belt from the floor he went to speak with his friend. Now they were all laughing as he started slapping the belt hard onto the table and looking over at her. "Soon she will be ours" He said to his friend. "To do with as we will, once the payment is satisfactory we shall be on our way with our magnificent new student. She will eventually be grateful to learn whatever we decide to teach her. Her benefactor is waiting to instruct her on the ways of man and as she has cost him a large amount of money she in turn has to repay him with many favours. He is not a greedy man and likes to share his fortune with his family. The family are fairly large with some uncles being a trifle larger than others. There are young cousins anxious to be shown how to use a female slave. She has to be waiting naked and ready to guide them into enjoying her, giving them much satisfaction. With our teachings she will do it well". He hesitated before saying. "I could feel her already wanting more of my tongue and I was enjoying penetrating deep into her throat and my Dick tells me it will be his turn for a deep search tomorrow, I am quite looking forward to it. Maybe friend if we rest her for five or ten minutes you could also play a tune on her tonsils. We don't want to overtire her and there is only one week in which to break her in, so we need to go steam ahead". The man helped Ann up, pulling back the hair from her face and sat her onto a chair. He took a couple of steps away, turning quickly and striking his hand hard across her face which sent her tumbling back down to the floor. Lifting her up again and sitting her onto the same chair he licked the tears from her hot battered face. "She has to learn the hard way; all slaves need a slap now and then". He began to laugh, and then continued with. "It will be just as hard for us being the teachers, as we cannot partake of the fresh juicy fruit. There are other female slaves in this establishment willing to full fill our needs but she has to stay a virgin for her master to break. You and I have a free hand with other matters". Ann knew they were discussing her but she was past caring it had been only yesterday she had met the man in the park and so many dreadful things had happened to her. The man continued speaking to his friend. "It will be a new experience for her learning what immense fun it can be. Her Master is very generous man and close friends will want to share his gift. Some are a little too young, as they have no facial hair yet but they will be allowed to watch and learn. We wouldn't stop them this is to be encouraged as it is their first step to becoming a man. Sharing between friends is good for all men and in this case some boys. She is a young strong Filly and beauty does not last long. There are always others getting ready to bud and starting to flower when they will be ripe for picking. It is now her time for deflowering and she will have to learn quickly or except the consequences which can be serious or final". Ann could feel someone close by her and now he was whispering into her ear and saying all the things he wanted to do to her, it was the man from the park. He had intended to do it earlier and would have if his interfering friends hadn't arrived and interrupted him. "You have come a long way since the park" He said. "It has been a great pleasure getting to know you. I know you will begin to enjoy pleasing and pleasuring so many friends. Not all at once that is impossible and you would need to practice more before you can take and enjoy a gang bang. The future is waiting for you; I only have one regret that I will not be amongst them. Like a fish you were caught in my net only to be served a dish for others. I will have to search for another young lady to share my picnic with. Don't you worry about me, I will not be using the same park again and this time she will be mine to have fun with." The two foreign men settled their account with the big man and told Ann to get dressed again and to wear warm clothing. The only warm clothes were her own school uniform and she was pleased to wear it. She was taken outside to a waiting van, it felt good to be out and she noted the number plate on a car that was standing there, she didn't know the make but she would remember it. Ann saw a long drive leading up to the house and two black Labrador dogs running in the grounds. Her head was aching, not only aching it was pounding. "You probably have a nasty headache". The big man said. "It's because you were given too much coffee" He laughed saying. "You silly girl that woman of mine gave you drugged coffee, you just can't trust anyone these days, can you?" The van doors opened and he said. "Now be off with you in you get and learn your lessons well. I believe you didn't like school so you can forget about all those lessons. Your new career is about to start and I have heard your new teacher can be very strict". The man was grinning and winked over to the van driver before continuing to say. "Your new master especially likes it if you are a little naughty then he can chastise you. I do believe you will learn to enjoy your new found profession and will eventually become very good at your trade. It may take a while for you to submit to the pleasures it can give to others but I know you will want to please your many admirers". Ann had no idea what the big man was talking about but she did know she was in serious trouble. She was pushed to the back of the van onto blankets and told to lie there, he fastened one of her hands to a steel ring on the side of the van and holding on to the other one he stretched his legs over her. Feeling his way under her skirt he began pushing his free hand between her legs. The driver called out to close the van door and lock it. The big man was slightly annoyed as he wanted to go much further and find out what she could offer. His woman was always watching him and he never got a chance to sample the fresh goods. "See what good fun it can be, when you learn to relax the fun will really start. Ask your owner for a line of the white stuff, if you're lucky you may get two and sniff it down deep. Fill your innards as if your lungs are about to burst then open your love channels to all the needy people who want to partake of them and allow their love to flow. Show them what a good slave you can be. If you disobey you will be beaten, if they have to chastise you it is because you are not doing what they ask you to do, be nice and they will love being with you. Always remember to please your master more than any other. What he wants you will give and do not try to escape or it could be a terrible punishment. Do as you are told and life will go easy, there is no way back. Good bye then, when your master has taught you all he knows and is in need of another bargain we may meet again and for that I would need a favour. Now that could prove to be interesting, I may ask your friend from the park if he would like to share my favour as he did become upset when my wife and I took you away from him. It's good to share with friends and he cannot help his feelings which you know he had for you. He is not good at controlling himself and sometimes he can go too far. He does regret what happens to his lady friends. He forgets all about it when he finds another and so it continues, one day he may be cured." The van door banged shut, they were off. No need to listen anymore she cried until she could cry no more and she was hurting. The drugs were wearing off and her head was pounding. The van jumped over the bumps in the road which didn't help with all her aches and pains. They must have been travelling for over two hours before they came to a stop and the doors were opened again. The driver climbed into the back and removed the lock and told her to get out. It was dark and the driver shone the torch as she clambered out of the van. "Stand there" He said. Ann didn't answer; she wasn't going to move anyway. In the dim light she could make out two figures moving toward them and as they got closer their voices told her one was a woman. She wondered if it could be the same woman who had bleached her hair but as they got nearer she could see it was a girl. She appeared to be around eighteen years old and she too had blonde hair. The person walking beside her was male; he wore riding boots and was holding two mean looking Alsatians which he had tethered together on one lead. A large gold chain hung around his neck and as he stretched out his hands to take hold of her, Ann couldn't help but notice the chunky gold rings decorating all his fingers. "Come here young lady." He said laughing and at the same time yanking her arm roughly. She could feel him scrutinising her. "You could do with a wash". He said. "Otherwise you are quite pleasing to the eye, but it's not only the eyes we need you to please now, is it?" The dogs were growling, he viciously kicked one and the other backed down wining. He passed Ann over to the girl saying "Get her cleaned up, fed and bed for the night, tomorrow we will show her how to earn her keep. Come on boys". He said raising his voice and tugging the dogs lead. We all could do with a good drink and a little tantalization". The two men from the van started talking loudly in a strange accent, joking and laughing with him...

Ann followed the blonde girl up the steps into a brightly lit room. The girl didn't speak to her but nudged her arm, which meant her to follow. They passed through a corridor with beautiful paintings on the wall. Ann had to look twice, the paintings may look beautiful but in every one an orgy was taking place and in the larger of the paintings it was all of women. The girl asked her name it was the first time she had spoken. Ann told her, she then asked what age she was and when Ann replied fourteen the girl looked shocked. "You are only a child" She said shaking her head in disbelief. "My name is Cindy and I will help you in any way I can. The only thing I cannot do is to help you to escape. We are prisoners here and those Alsatians can be nasty. They are like pussy cats compared to the others ones he has". She held open a door for Ann to go through and she stepped into a bedroom which could have been from one of those expensive hotels she had seen on film. "This will be your room" Cindy said. "Over here is your bath and shower room and there are lots of perfumes waiting for you" She took a tape measure from her pocket and proceeded to take Ann's measurements. "We have a wardrobe with all the latest fashions and as you are a size ten there is a vast choice. While you bathe I will fetch you something to wear tomorrow when you will meet the family. Do you have a preference for colour?" She asked. "No" answered Ann. "I don't want to wear any of them". Cindy screwed up her face before saying "I wish you would because if you don't try to make yourself alluring then both of us are going to be in a lot of trouble. They kidnapped you, which was a horrid situation to be in and still must be. As for me I knew what I was getting into my eyes were wide and greedy. The comfort of living in luxury and being given beautiful clothes to wear and not paying for anything was tempting and I took the bait. This house is a step down from a palace with a devil to rule it. I believed it would be better than walking the streets. I didn't realize they would keep me a prisoner and there would be no way out of this Palace / Mausoleum. She turned off the bath taps saying. "Do as they say and maybe one day you will find a way out, it's your only hope". The steam was rising from the bath tub and the aromas of roses and lavender drifted around the room, all the sweet scents from a garden. Ann couldn't resist she needed to feel the cleansing bubbles and wash the dirt away. Stepping into the bath she slid down and let the water soak over her head. Ann lay under the warmth of the bubbles letting the water envelope her. She held her breath not wanting to rise back up to the surface. Bubbles escaped from her mouth making her gasp for air and her head lifted clear. Cindy was back in the room holding a large towel. "Are you ready to come out?" she asked. Ann slid back under the water then up again shaking her long blonde hair and spreading the water everywhere. "Would you mind if I enjoyed bathing a little longer?" She asked Cindy adding a big smile. "Another ten minutes should be alright". She answered back. "I will leave you for a while". She laid the towel on a chair and was gone. Once more the bubbles rose over her head comforting, cuddling and Ann wanted to stay there safe like a baby back in the womb. Her head felt heavy, too heavy to lift and she was sleepy so very sleepy and it felt as though she was drifting away, was she floating? A haze gathered close around her and she felt a wonderful feeling of contentment and peace. Ann looked at the bath tub and the face down in the water with hair sprayed out like a silken blanket, it was---herself. It didn't shock her why should it? She didn't hurt nor was she afraid and they couldn't touch her now. She felt sorry for Cindy, what was going to happen to her? She was getting the blame for leaving her in the bath alone. Cindy was lying on the floor doubled up and holding her stomach crying. What could she do to help her? She had never been dead before it wasn't the sort of thing one could try before buying. Ann watched as they lifted her body and dropped it onto the large towel, the one that Cindy had brought for her to dry herself on and rolled it tightly around her. The man with the rings brought a heavy plastic bag and held it open whilst the other men pushed her in. "Take the bitch out to the van and get rid of her" He shouted. "Where are we going to dump her?" The van driver enquired. "Find somewhere, anywhere." The boss man yelled back. "I don't give a damn where you stick the sick bitch as long as she is off my doorstep". He put his foot into Cindy as he left the room grimacing at her. "I will sort you out later". He said. As an afterthought he stepped back into the room saying. "You have lost me a hell of a lot of money and you had better be ready to double your workload". He pushed his foot once more at her buttocks, kicking Cindy and sending her sliding over the wet floor. He shouted loudly at her "Clean this bloody place up". As he finally walked from the room. The men carried the plastic bag out to the van. Ann didn't follow there was no need; she knew where to find herself. How would her mother know where she was? If only she could turn back time and go back to school with her friends and be with her mother again. She sighed, knowing that it couldn't be. Cindy stood up rubbing a big mark on the side of her face and still crying. "Oh Ann" She said between sobs.

"Why did you have to do it?" Ann wished she could tell her she hadn't wanted to cause trouble she had only wanted to get away. Cindy began to clean the bathroom knowing that all traces of the young girl had to be removed. Ann noticed a button which had been pulled off her school skirt on the floor. Cindy picked it up holding it in both palms with her eyes closed as if in prayer. Ann knew she had to let Cindy know she was still here. Suddenly the button was thrown across the room and Cindy was shaking her hands as if they were on fire. The button was red hot and spinning around in circles. Even though Cindy's hands were burning it was nothing compared to the patterns being written in the suds on the floor? "Ann will help you, don't be afraid". Cindy couldn't believe what she was seeing, was she going mad? When she looked again it was only bubbles on the floor. She bent down picking the button up again turning it over in her hands, it was cold and wet.

Ann had found a way of contacting Cindy and she was determined to find each one of the paedophiles' who had been so vile with her and probably others before her. First on the list was the boss man, she had to stop him from assaulting Cindy anymore and make him pay for his nasty wicked ways. A little at a time would be sufficient until he could see his empire crumble before him. Then his own hand would deal the final blow. Ann could see him with the van driver in deep conversation. He must have got rid of her quickly as her body was not in the van. He was patting the driver on the back and smiling, which meant for sure her remains would never be seen again. She realized now when they spoke about the pig farm they were speaking the truth, especially as it was almost on their doorstep. If they ate pork they could be eating her. Now she was getting morbid and she should be thinking of revenge not only for herself but for the others and Cindy. The boss man banged shut one van door and as he slammed the other one his heavy gold chain swung and got caught in a hinge. His feet tripped as he was pulled with the door and the chain tightened around his neck choking him. The driver rushed to his aid but couldn't break the hold. He shouted for help and two men came running. Seeing it was a situation of life or death one of the men applied cutters to the chain. It may have been luck or a week link in the chain. It did give way and the man could breathe again. He was not pleased as his neck was hurting, the cutters had taken chunks out and the blood was everywhere He couldn't shout his throat was sore, he wanted to kill someone. Ann Laughed. "This is only the beginning". She said, but no one could hear her. The men helped their boss back into his pretentious palace to recover from his ordeal and a doctor was called. Ann could tell the men were scared as their boss would eventually blame one of them. They put their heads together deciding what story or excuse they could say but how could they find one, it was an accident. Cindy knew the doctor had been called and the boss had been close to death with choking. She was scared as he could vent his anger on anyone. She knew too that the spirit of Ann was around because she had left her a message in the bubbles. At the time she was uncertain as the weird happening with the button spooked her and then came the writing. "Thank you Ann" She said. "I may sound crazy perhaps I am but I can feel you here. I know things will be alright". A cold shiver came over Cindy making the hairs on her arms stand straight. It was Ann's way of showing she was not gone and Cindy knew. Ann was starting to enjoy being a Spirit she had never realized how much could be achieved in a few hours. The next on her agenda had to be the sweet pretender from the park and the place to look was in the parks. If she found his car she would find him. Travelling wasn't easy; there was some sort of barrier keeping her in the area where she had died. She pushed hard shoving against the invisible wall and nothing budged. "I need to get there" She cried. "I need to stop him".

Suddenly, it was as if curtains had been opened up and she found herself standing outside of park gates. She moved through and could see his car parked in a far corner. Ann had never been in this park before but it seemed that he had because the ice crème lady was saying how nice it was to see him and did he want one or two cornets to day. "I think I will take two". He answered. "My daughter is coming to meet me and she is going to want one. If she doesn't arrive soon I shall have to eat it before it melts" The lady handed two ices to him saying "Enjoy them, go on eat them both". He smiled at her, which he was good at and strolled away. Finding a bench he sat down waiting. The ice crèmes were melting and he was having to lick his hands clean and at the same time he was watching a girl doing skipping exercisers in her shorts. Ann was watching too and would have enjoyed a lick of the ice crème and she wasn't alone. Overhead the tree was swarming with insect's busy building a wasp nest. They were interesting creatures and it was amazing to see the wonderful structure they were building. You had to be very careful because a little disturbance would make them angry and they do love ice crème. Closing her eyes she moved her thoughts onto the nest. Nothing seemed to happen until the man dropped a cornet onto the ground. This annoyed him and he kicked it. A couple of the insects were tasting the sweetness and buzzed angrily. One of the wasps began circling the man in frenzy. The other wasps thought they were being attacked and joined in. Hundreds of them massed together flying onto the head of the man first and eventually covering all of his body. He was flaying his arms and screaming loudly in pain. The girl who had been skipping ran to the ice crème lady and stayed in her van, there was nothing they could do to help. When the police arrived the man was dead from shock and as they said later, they had been looking for him as he was notorious for trying to pick up young girls and he wouldn't be missed. Ann was relieved knowing that dreadful man couldn't hurt girls ever again. It wasn't nice the way he had met his end but his wicked ways had brought this about and he did anger the wasps. She would go back to see Cindy and hope the boss man was still suffering. The Alsatians' were tied up and for the first time Ann felt sorry for them. They both looked cold and hungry and forgotten about. The two of them were lying on wet muddy ground and one was whimpering whilst trying to lick an open wound on its leg. Ann remembered seeing the boss man kicking the animals, so they were never well treated. Looking through one of the windows Ann could see the driver and his other friends eating and drinking, they were having a social evening. A game of cards was on the table Ann noticed the van driver's cards as she entered the room and he appeared to be winning. She remembered watching a film where trouble had started because one of the players dropped a card under a table. Being a spirit had its good side she could see them and they couldn't see her. She moved over to the card table and with her fingers manoeuvred the card onto the floor, dropping it behind his feet. The driver was laughing and threw his cards onto the table and started thumping it, he had won the game. Standing up he began to count his winnings. The sulk on the other men's faces showed how surprised and annoyed they were. They slammed their cards down and moved away. One of the men said something to the other three and spat onto the ground. Picking up a bottle of whisky he poured himself a drink, dropping the top of the bottle onto the floor. Ann blew on it gently and it rolled further beneath the table. She was expecting the man to bend and retrieve it but he didn't seem to be bothered. His glass was empty and he began drinking from the bottle taking a good swig before putting it down onto the table again. One of his friends reached out for the whisky but the man pushed in front of him to snatch it. They lost their balance and fell drunkenly under the table. There in front of them was a card lying face upwards, "The Ace of Spades" with the top of the whisky bottle holding it down like a paper weight. The two men were slightly drunk, one more than the other but not too far gone to know that the driver had been cheating, why else would that card be under the table? There language was horrendous to Ann's ears, because even though she couldn't understand them their noise was overwhelming and made her cringe. The third man had his arm around the driver's neck holding him tight. One of the drunks was holding a gun to the side of his head shouting and screaming into the drivers face. Ann had heard and seen enough but as she moved away she heard a gun shot then all fell silent, only the smell of sulphur filled the air.

Cindy wondered what was happening but was too afraid to show herself. She had heard gunshots before and had been warned to keep her nose out. This time was different as the boss man was too sick for it to have been him. The dogs were growling as she passed them and she threw a couple of bones in their direction, they stopped growling and became quiet. Cindy pulled herself back quickly into a dark corner as some of the men who worked there were almost rolling out of their drinking den and dragging the man who drove the van behind them. Could they have shot him? She was scared; if they saw her she could be next. The way his head was dropped over was a sure sign he was dead. She couldn't see any blood and didn't want to either anyway it was too dark. They moved out of her sight pulling him by his legs, one was holding a torch in front of them. The further away they got the light became dimmer, until Cindy couldn't see the light anymore. Being careful to avoid the dogs she went indoors and back to her own rooms, she wasn't safe there but she felt as though she was. The house phone was ringing and Cindy answered it. "Where the hell have you been? I've rang you twice and I want more pain killers and when I'm well again you will get my boot up your arse. Hurry up and get here before I think of something else I can give you". It was the boss man and he slammed the phone down. Ann was there watching Cindy as she hurriedly moved to the bosses apartments, she could almost feel her fear. As she opened his door Ann moved in with her blowing warm air onto her face. The only effect it had on Cindy was for her to hold her breath. She had no idea Ann was there. "Get here" The boss said while pointing to his neck. "Change this bloody bandage and be quick with my pills". The bandage had the odour of a dead animal and as Cindy unwrapped it the worse it smelt, underneath was black in colour. "You bitch you are pressing too hard" He said. "Get your hands off me, give me my pills and get the doctor". He tried to hit her but missed and started shouting. "Go on get those damned pills now". This time Ann could help, the pills were in a box marked two every four hours. Ann flicked her eyes and the numbers moved around making it four every two hours. Cindy helped him to take them and he swallowed them without question along with a big drink of his whisky. It was gone in a swig and he threw the glass at Cindy breaking it against her arm, she flinched as the splinters cut into her flesh causing the blood to flow onto her hand. "Get another glass" He shouted. "And don't get that mess all over it, hurry up move yourself". Cindy quickly went to fetch another glass but she felt faint and the dizziness was making her head spin. Moving over to the door she opened it wide for air forgetting that the dogs were outside. Picking up a glass she hurried back to the boss man who was laid in an awkward position in his chair. His head was lolling over and his arm was dangling over the side. Cindy walked around to the front of him and he was still breathing, although she hated him she was glad she hadn't hasted his death and he was still alright. She left the building without looking back hoping she wouldn't bump into the others as they all seemed drunk and she had heard a shot. Reaching her own apartments Cindy threw herself down onto the bed and wept, without cleaning her cut arm. There was nothing Ann could do to help, Cindy had to get it out of her system and learn how to fight these criminals. There was a lot of noise outside with dogs barking, men shouting and the screaming was horrendous. Hearing this Cindy jumped off the bed to see what the commotion could be, it was fairly dark and she couldn't see what was happening. The lights for the front of the building were on a main switch above her head, standing on a chair she pulled the lever down and the whole of the grounds was flooded in bright light, the scene below her was a sea of red. The dogs were attacking their master, they must have pulled him off his chair and out into the grounds. They were hungry and he was available, the men were trying to beat them off and only succeeded in making them more annoyed. One of the men had a nasty injury to his leg, he couldn't stand and dragged himself away leaving the other two trying to help their boss. Cindy could tell that the boss man was dead as he was torn limb from limb, the dogs must have really hated him. The remaining two men beat their way back through the main doors with the animals following and slammed the doors behind them. They both collapsed on the floor leaving the dogs barking wildly outside. Ann watched as Cindy stood staring when she should be getting away from this hell, she wanted to shake her and awaken her from this state but she didn't move. Although Ann was a lot younger than Cindy being deceased had given her maturity and an ability to think for others when they couldn't do it for themselves. Closing her eyes Ann thought hard forcing words into her friends head telling her to get out while she had the chance. It was working because Cindy reached out taking a warm coat and her bag from the wardrobe. She took some money she had been saving and stuffed it into her bag plus all the fancy gold necklaces and rings they had made her wear to please the others. The back door was the way out as the men were in the front of the house and wouldn't see her leave. There was the other man somewhere around who she would have to avoid, maybe if she cut across the fields it would lead to the main road where she could get help. She would need her boots, the only ones she had were with heels which would be bloody useless. The gardeners hut was close by and Cindy knew she would find rubber boots in there, hopefully they will fit. Ann couldn't warn her friend she already knew the other man had crawled into there to avoid the dogs and Cindy was just about to open the hut door. A moan made Cindy jump back, someone was in there but she still needed boots. Picking up a lump of wood she quietly opened the door and there on the floor lay the man. He lifted his head to look at her and groaned in pain, his hand took hold of her ankle and she kicked him off. She had no pity, he didn't deserve any. There was a row of boots in the far corner all turned upside down to dry, Cindy found a pair that fitted. Ann was becoming impatient as Cindy was taking too long and if any others came along she could be caught. There was a sound of gun shots and then of a dog howling, another shot and silence. The men had killed the dogs and would soon be looking for her, after they had got rid of the mutilated body. At last Cindy was moving into the fields, she had no idea which way to go all she wanted was to get as far away from this place as she could. It was so muddy, she laughed to herself and imagined what it would have been like in her high heels, funny that was something she hadn't done for a long time. As she trudged through the fields she started to think about Ann and how young and sweet she was and what about her mother? She must still be looking for her not knowing where she is or what has happened to her. Only she knew the dreadful truth and one day Cindy vowed, she would tell her mother everything that happened. Ann picked up the feelings from Cindy and it pleased her knowing her mother would find her resting place. The one thing the men did in her favour was not to drop her down a deep well or feed her to the pigs. Her mother often made roast pork dinner and it could have been her, ugh, what a horrid thought. Her friend was climbing over a gate into another field, how many more gates would she have to pass through before she found a road. Cindy felt this was the right direction, maybe Ann was guiding her. It started raining and the mud was getting thicker, her hair was sticking to her face she was cold and tired. There was nothing Ann could do to help, another couple of fields and she would come across a small road leading to a motor way, if only she keeps on going. Cindy could see lights in front of her so there was a road. "If you can hear me Ann" She said. "Thank you for helping me and showing me where to find my way, I only wish that I could have helped you". She hesitated before saying. "I will never forget you, in the short time we were together there was a bond between us like sisters and I will find your mother". If Ann could have cried she would have but time on earth was too short now and there was things she had to do whilst she was still able. The last gate and Cindy fell against it shouting "We made it Ann, were here and over there I can see the motor way". Ann wasn't listening she was already on her way to where the man from the park her kidnapper, had first taken her. If she listened carefully she could hone in on the Labradors vibrations, it should be easy for her to find. "Found it" Ann was pleased. "There's that lovely farm house with those pretty chickens, how unfair". She watched as the chickens went about their daily pickings. "It is the only problem they have to solve, how easy their life is". The house was not to blame she thought, with new owners it could be a beautiful home again. There was only the man and woman living there and after the park man had been stung to death they had to be informed, being his only relatives. The Police had re opened investigations after the macabre accident, all the trails left behind of his abductions seemed to end in this area. Two police cars stood where Ann had been chained in the van and as she watched the man and his wife came outside in handcuffs and got into separate cars. Another police van arrived with more officers and they all entered the farm house apart from one officer who went to see the animals. Ann could hear he was ringing for animal protectors' to look after them. The man and his wife from the farm were bad but their animals were well cared for. Unlike the boss man from the big house who starved his dogs to make them vicious and at the end they showed him how vicious they could be. The two cars sped off taking the pair with them, leaving behind other officers to search the premises. Nothing that Ann could do here the Police would find everything out eventually. She wondered if Cindy had found help, it was time she went to find her. Cindy had left the fields and she was grateful for the boots for without them she wouldn't have made it this far, the ploughed fields made the going tough. A couple of cars had passed by without seeing her but then she was afraid of showing herself in case they were from the house. She knew she would have to take a chance as it was the only way to get any help and without it Ann's mother would never know about her daughter. "Ann" Cindy said through tears. "I wish you were here and none of these horrid things had ever happened. You would be alive again and we would have been real friends". She paused another car was coming, this was it she had to wave it down. She lost her nerve again and the car sped on past, what was she to do? Ann was with her now and she too was wondering how to get her out of this dilemma. Looking toward the fields Ann noticed two horses leaning over a gate, if she could spook them into the road it should be enough to stop a car. First she had to get the gate open which wouldn't be easy. It needed immense pressure of thought to move it, she was successful and in doing so the horses walked through onto the roadside. Ann was pleased not having to spook the animals, they had left the field simply because the way out was open for them. Cindy hadn't noticed them as she was watching the other side of the road and listening, she could hear another car in the distance. Ann nipped the ear of one horse and he shook his head she then pulled hard on his tail and he kicked up his back legs in annoyance. The other horse seemed perplexed as to what was upsetting his stable mate and wanted to get away, he cantered into the road lingering there in the centre until a cars headlights startled him. He froze for a moment, then galloped off. The car came to a stop and a man got out, he seemed very annoyed. Cindy was rooted to the spot as the man walked over to where she stood. "What the hell do you think you are doing?" He almost spat the words at her. "You should keep your horses tethered not strolling around a darkened road where they can cause a nasty accident" He paused and looked at her, she was acting strange. "Did you hear what I said to you?" He was standing up close and could see the fear in her face which made him feel sorry for shouting at her. "Let me give you a lift to where you are going, it's a long way to the nearest town and I promise I will not shout at you anymore. All you need to do is tell me where you want to go". Cindy didn't answer. He could take her to the nearest town and let the police deal with her as for the horses he could put them back into a field and let their owner find them. They were lucky they hadn't been injured and himself too, what a damned nuisance it was but he couldn't just leave them on the roadside. Shining the car lights onto the horses he got behind them and started shooing them back through the gate, seeing the grass they both went in easily. Taking Cindy by the hand he asked. "Will you allow me to try to help you?" She answered this time with a nod of her head, after hearing a voice telling her to get in. Ann couldn't think of how else to make her get into the car. She wouldn't sit in the front seat and the driver didn't mind as she wasn't easy to talk to. The quicker he found someplace to drop her off he would feel his duty was done. It took less than ten minutes for her to fall asleep and another three quarters of an hour before he sighted lights from a town in the distance. He breathed a sigh of relief soon he would be able to hand her over. The road widened and the smell of civilisation filled the air, moving further into the town he spotted a lone policeman and opened his window wide to speak with him. He explained the situation to the officer who listened intently before bending and peering through the window to look at the sleeping girl. He took out a note book and scribbled in it before directing him to the police station. Driving the car down the main road he turned into a side street where the blue lamp hung in the Police station entrance, they were here. The girl was stirring he was glad she would be able to explain her own story, that's if she knew it. It was nothing to do with him she could sort herself out. "I see your awake now" He said to her leaning over and helping her out of the car. Candy got out and looked around. "Where are we?" She asked. He answered her saying. "We are at a police station and I am sure they will be able to assist you much better than I can. This is as far as I can go and I will have to leave you here. So if you get out now I will tell the police where I found you and be on my way". She got out but he was sure she wasn't listening to him, her face was blank. Up the steps into the station, choosing a seat by the counter to sit on and staring at the woman behind it. "Hello" The female officer said and continued with. "Would you tell me the reason why you are here"? Cindy had been in a place like this before, her head was aching. What was she doing here? Her thoughts were banging inside her head. She could recall the house and the flight through the fields in rubber boots and that man in the shed, she couldn't forget him. That man talking to the police woman he had held her hand and brought her here. Her thoughts were playing havoc with her mind. Someone handed her a glass of water, she was grateful and the coolness of the ice soothed her aching head. The car driver was saying his goodbyes when Cindy grabbed his jacket. "Don't go, please don't go". She was pleading with him to stay, why? He didn't know but he knew he couldn't refuse her. He sat himself down beside her and the police officer came out from behind the desk. She knew there was something else she needed telling and from the way the girl had been behaving it could be serious. What was said next astounded both of them. "They killed my friend she was only fourteen and they let her die, they killed her, they killed her". Cindy couldn't breathe she was gasping for air and the man was telling her to calm down. The officer called for help and two males came in quickly taking Cindy into another room to lie down whilst a doctor was called. "Excuse me Sir" The police officer behind the desk said. "From what the young girl has told us our enquiries are going to have to dig a lot deeper" The driver of the car moved over to the desk saying. "I understand, if what she says is true then of cause you will have to ask more questions. Let me assure you" He continued "This has absolutely nothing to do with me all I did was bring her here and you know the rest". Another officer took him into a small room where once again he was questioned as to why he had picked her up. "We need some identification from you" The officer said. "Your driver's license should suffice". The man pulled his wallet out and threw it down onto the desk. "I am now under suspicion for murder which neither of us know to be true and all I did was help this young girl, so much for doing a good deed". "We are sorry if we gave you this impression sir" The officer answered. "We have our duty to perform as you were with the said person at the time she entered the station. We have to reaffirm the name and address that you gave us is you're actual identity". The wallet laid on the desk and the officer asked him to take out his license and hand it to him. "Your name is?" The officer asked. "Gerald Bourne" The man replied. All the questions he had answered before were checked. "You can go now sir and thank you for your assistance, we may call upon your help later with our enquiries" He held out his hand to shake and Gerald shook it, it wasn't the police man's fault he had his work to do. "If you don't mind officer I would like to know if the girl's story is true, she did ask me to stay" "Of cause you can" The answer came back. "It may take a while so make yourself a drink the kettle is already on the boil and there's tea or coffee, help yourself". The officer left him in the room it was going to be a long waiting time. He made a coffee and sat there wondering what the girl's story was all about, could it be true someone had been killed? It was no wonder she was so traumatised.

Ann had stayed around until she knew her friend was in safe hands and now she was going back to the house. She laughed to herself. "I always believed dead people couldn't leave the place they died in. Adults make up such a load of rubbish because I can go where ever I want to go". She had to find out if those three men were still around. "One may still be in the shed" She said to herself "He wasn't capable of going anywhere very fast". Ann laughed louder than ever, it didn't matter as no one could hear her. It was time for her to get the other two. It was an easy task getting there travelling at speed was an amazing feeling and the house seemed peaceful now. The beautiful alluring gardens were alive and buzzing with the sounds of birds and bees, she had never noticed these wonderful things before and it had taken until now for her to appreciate them. There was no sign of the boss man's body or what had happened to it, the dogs too had vanished. A strong smell of bleach came from where the body had lain and it was making Ann feel dizzy. She realized the smell was affecting her, bleach was not good. She didn't know why but she had to get away from the aroma. The air was clearer at the back of the house and even there she couldn't pick up the scent of the two men. "Their smell has to be around this place". She thought. "Their minds alone were like sewers on a hot day". Ann was puzzled... A breeze blew across her face and she smiled welcoming its soft touch onto her spirit body. Her face screwed up in disgust when a pong from the men filled her nostrils. She had found them all she had to do was follow the scent. Here they were drunk as usual it was the strong smell of bleach which had covered their hiding place. She had to be careful of bleach as it could stop her from being here, she had felt dizzy and the world around her had started fading away. Ann knew eventually she would have to leave this world behind but not before these men suffered for their nasty ways and she had to be sure that her dear mother would know where to find her. "I am going to take a piss" The fatter of the two said and struggled to stand up falling onto his friend. "Be bloody careful you fool" The other man growled at him. "I don't want your waste products sprayed over me". Ann was seeing a way of getting to them and the drink was helping. "It wouldn't take much for them to become annoyed with each other and with a little help from herself maybe the sparks will fly". The ideas were running through her head. "Of cause, the horses". She was speaking to herself again. "If I can persuade them to leave the field and follow me we may be able to trap the men inside until the Law arrives. I am sure they can't be far away as Cindy has told them the story. They are bound to investigate as soon as possible". A great deal of thought was running through Ann's head. Altogether there were five men at the house including the boss man. Two of them were dead, one was injured and the two drunks were still in there but what had happened to the foreign men who had paid money to buy her, they seem to have disappeared from the scene. That would be her next mission to find them but her first one was to make sure the drunks didn't get away from their just deserts. The two horses were grazing and when Ann got closer one shook his head and whinnied while the other galloped off. Ann realized she was scaring them, humans cannot see what animals can. She knew if she stood still they would become inquisitive and lose their fear. "Everyone and everything is afraid of the unknown". Ann said to herself. She began to think about her mother and what she would be thinking, by now the police must have informed her about what had happened to her daughter. It had been her own fault if she had only listened but she had been too headstrong to take advice from anybody, least of all her mother. The horses were coming nearer and Ann was coxing them into following her, both of them moved in closely behind her heels. How she would have loved to stroke their beautiful dark manes, their hair was the same colour as hers used to be. Ann looked at her hair and it was back to its original colour, she was so surprised. It would have pleased her mother to see her looking this way as she wouldn't have liked that bleached tarty appearance of her as a blonde and she wasn't old enough to dye her hair. What was she thinking about her mother will never wash or comb her hair again, she had to stop feeling sorry for herself there was work to do. The horses and Ann were standing in front of the house when the larger of the men opened the door. "Bloody hell you drunken git, come see what we got here". He shouted to his mate inside of the room. "Sod off" Was the answer. "Who you calling a drunk you want to look at yourself first". He threw the bottle of whiskey onto the floor, he'd had enough anyway. "Come on quick before they go" The bigger man shouted. "I'm here now what's up with you". He stopped in his tracks before saying. "Who let these out of the field? These are the bloody studs that sire the mares for the racing stables. Our foreign governor's will not be happy if they go missing". He continued saying "They are worth more money than any blonde bimbo could make". He walked over to the horses and patted both of them before turning his head toward his friend and asking "Where did you put the blonde bitch anyway? We don't want her popping up and upsetting our applecart. If the big boys find out what happened to her we can blame it onto the Boss and his bad temper and say he scarpered before they found out". His mate nodded in agreement saying. "All the mess is cleaned up especially the girl she was laid to rest". He paused and laughed as though he was telling a joke and continued with. "The stupid bitch is laying with an old farmer and probably doing her duty down under. We put her into a newly dug grave and there were plenty of flowers so she had a good send-off" He sniggered before saying "Some people are so lucky". His friend was leading the horses away. "I am going to put these two into the stable where we can be sure they will be safe, you could go and find the other bitch that works here and make sure she knows the story to tell if she's asked. He continued with. "She's probably hiding in her room". The first man laughed again saying. "She won't stay in hiding long and when I find her I will need some satisfaction for all the trouble she has caused me in looking for her". His friend called back. "You're a dirty old man and I know what your satisfaction means, go on and enjoy yourself. I have these animals to bed down". Ann was appalled these men couldn't be human, he could search all night and he wouldn't find

Cindy but Ann knew where to find him. She watched as he filled their buckets with water and fastened up their feed bags. He threw blankets over their backs and patted them whilst speaking gently in a soft voice. "Unbelievable". Thought Ann it was a surprise for her seeing the horses being well treated, she hadn't expected this of him. But was he ready to be taken care of? It was time for him to pay his penance. He was smoothing the back end of the full stallion when Ann blew into the horses ear making him rear up. "Steady boy" the man said "Must be something here spooking you ". Little did he know how true his words were? He moved over to the next stall where the yearling stood and Ann followed. This time she blew into the horses nostrils and the animal became excited. The man couldn't understand why this was happening. "Stop it boy, what's wrong with both of you? Anyone would think you had seen a ghost". The yearling calmed down as he stroked his nozzle. "You're ok now" He said walking to the back of the stall. "I will see you both in the morning". The young horse kicked out his back legs and sent him flying into the other stall. He managed to get to his feet before the stallion in the other stall lifted his hind quarters and his hooves connected with the man kicking him high into the air. He fell back down, head first onto the end of a sharp implement used for cleaning the stables. Ann didn't look, the man had now paid his penance.

Inside of the house the fatter man was still searching for the girl Cindy. "What if the bitch has run away? She may have seen what happened to the boss and got scared, we should have caged the trollop before she got the chance". He was becoming angrier by the minute there wasn't any sign of her in the house, he decided to try the sheds outside. "I am going to break her neck when I find her". He muttered. Over at the stables all seemed quiet and he wondered what was keeping his friend so long. "While bedding down those horses he probably thinks I am bedding the girl and he is taking his time for me to enjoy it. Shit!" He exclaimed "I will kill the bitch for taking the piss" He tried a couple of the sheds slamming the doors hard with no success. The gardeners hut was different, things thrown around and he could hear a slight sound like heavy breathing. Taking out his gun he moved towards the door "She is going to regret making me into a fool, nobody takes the mickey out of me and gets away with it". He kicked hard and the hut door opened wide. A movement from under some garden sacks told him she was there. "Come out you stupid bitch I am waiting to make you dance" She didn't move and he shouted again. "Come out now or you will be sorry". The sacks moved a little but no one came from under them. "Stay there then if that's what you want". The man raised his gun and shot into the sacks twice. Saying. "Too bad stupid cow, she was getting too old anyway but she was a good fuck, he would miss her". With his foot he lifted the sacks to take his last look at the body beneath. His mouth dropped wide open as he sucked in his breath with the shock. It was the van driver who had cheated at cards, he was dead now for sure. They hadn't done a good job on him before and he could have come back and done a lot of damage. "Gosh they were lucky" He breathed a sigh of relief. "Wait until I tell my mate, he's never going to believe me". He walked away from the scene toward the stables before he realized he still had not found the missing girl. "Bloody hell. He said. She's got to be found, she knows too much". Reaching the stable door he called out his friends name loudly, once more he shouted but got no answer. Stepping inside he could see the horses tethered to their stalls. "Where the hell is he?" Scratching his head puzzled he turned to go out and tripped over a fork handle sticking out of a bundle of hay. "Clumsy dicks" He moaned. "Fucking leaving these things strewn all over the floor". Bending to pick it up he saw blood mixed into the straw. Pulling the straw away disclosed a pool of blood with his friend sprawled out lifeless and his face unrecognizable. Looking closer he could see where the stalls were smashed and it seemed as though the horses had gone into some sort of frenzy and kicked him to death. "Shit; I'm getting out of this place before anything else happens. It's just me and the girl now, when Ifind her". He was shaking, something had turned really bad since that girl had drowned. It was as if she had put a curse on them like the mummies of old. The boss had died and not in a very nice way also his two mates, although one was his fault he had shot him. He was having second thoughts about finding the girl. "Fuck the bitch". He spat out. "Let her rot, if I can't find her maybe the curse will". The van was still standing outside and he hurried over to it. Taking his last look at the house he got in and turned the engine, it purred into life. He was off. Ann watched him go, time would catch up with him eventually she was going back to the police station to see what was happening with Cindy.

The station was abuzz with activity, police officers moving in and out of rooms talking on their mobiles and others outside sitting in their squad cars waiting for the start signal to go. Cindy was sat crying in the arms of a woman who too appeared to be crying. The woman was stroking her hair, it reminded Ann of having her own hair stroked when she sat watching television at her mother's feet. There was something similar about the female she could feel a pull as though she was being moved toward the two of them. The woman held Cindy by the shoulders bending in and kissing her on the cheek and then wiping away Cindy's tears before her own. Ann couldn't believe what she was seeing it was her mother she wanted to cry out and tell her she was here but she couldn't. Ann knew her mother would keep searching for her and she was glad knowing Cindy had found her. A man was introducing himself to her mother, she turned to listen. "Sorry". He said. "I don't want to intrude". Ann's mother held out her hand and smiled. "You're not intruding Mr" She hesitated smiling again and continued with. "It's my turn to say sorry as I don't know your name". "My name is Gerald Bourne" He answered shaking her hand. "I only wanted to say that I was the person who picked up this young lady in my car. She was in a sorry state dazed and alone on a lonely road that was the reason I brought her to this place. I had no idea at the time about your missing daughter but I know where I picked this young lady up. I have to go now to help the police with their investigations I shall be able show them the exact place where I found her". A plain clothed detective entered the room, he nodded to Ann's mother and said to Gerald "We are almost ready for off Sir, so if there is any more information you can give to us apart from what we already know it could be useful". Gerald Bourne shook his head saying. "No". "There may be a tiny bit tucked away in your memory" The detective answered. "However small it may be". He paused, clearing his throat and continued. "We would be grateful for anything you can remember." Gerald shook his head again. "I have told you as much as I know if there is anything I can think of on the way I will certainly tell you." Gerald turned to the ladies saying. "I hope to see you both later and be bringing news that will help in the search for Ann your friend". He took hold of Ann's mothers hand and said. "I will pray to find your beloved daughter". Saying his goodbyes he followed the detective outside. Two police vans filled with officers were behind the detective's car and Gerald travelled in the back with the detectives in the front seat. The country roads were winding and at a blind bend a large white van came speeding around the corner. Immediately the police car and the ones behind pulled quickly into the verge, otherwise it may have been a severe accident. The detective was swiftly on his phone. "Stop that bloody idiot" He yelled down it. "He almost caused a crash. He stopped to catch his breath before saying. "I'll make sure they throw the book at him". They stayed at the side of the road until an officer reported the offender had been apprehended and was being taken into custody. "I'll deal with him later" The detective said. "We have more important things to sort out first". Telling his driver to start the car they moved out onto the road. Gerald was busy watching the scenery, one field looked like the rest and he hadn't taken much notice of the surrounds as he had been busy with the horses and the girl. "Could it be here"? He questioned himself. "Can you stop the car?" Gerald called out, turning his head to the rear something he had seen jogged his memory. He was almost sure it was the gate where the horses had got onto the road. The car pulled up abruptly. "Is this the place then?" The detective asked. "I believe it is". Gerald answered. "Good" The detective declared and went to give his officers instructions. One by one Gerald could see them spreading like ants all over the fields, searching as they went. Gerald was left sitting in the car wondering why they had needed his help if they were going to leave him sitting there. He needn't have worried because the detective came over and offered him some boots to wear. "There to keep your feet dry" He said. "I bet you thought we had forgotten about you, tell the truth now you did didn't you?" The detective was laughing as Gerald looked a trifle embarrassed. With the boots on and jacket zipped he followed the detective into the field. They were heading toward a large farm house and the detective was explaining on the way that it had been turned into one of these palatial residents for foreign gentry. "I've sent a couple of officers ahead without their dogs". He said. "Got to be careful" He continued "As they too could be keeping dogs on their premises. The men are able to look after themselves but I insisted on them wearing protective clothing just in case animals are guarding the place". It started to rain and Gerald realized that being a police man was not what he had imagined it would be. Some of the officers were in the tall grass searching on their knees. "What are they all looking for?" He asked. "If I knew I would tell you" The answer came back. "We have been suspicious of the owners for some time and their comings and goings and now there is a missing girl involved". Gerald interrupted him. "Don't you mean a murdered girl "? The detective answered him saying. "This is not what I am saying sir, we do not have a body nor proof of a murder and until we do she stays as missing". Ann was listening to them. "Cindy had already told him she was dead was he ignorant, what other proof did he need"? She thought about causing him to slip and fall in the mud but that would be stupid, he was after all trying to find the guilty people and the truth about her disappearance. It all takes time and Ann knew she had lots of that. Gerald hadn't said anything to the detective for a good ten minutes and now they were in the grounds of the house. He had been asking too many questions and the detective had answered him in a rather abrupt manner and according to protocol this meant shut up. "You have gone quiet" The detective was speaking again. "I thought you were busy deciding your next move and I didn't want to interrupt". Gerald replied. That was untrue as Gerald really believed he was getting on the other mans nerves. "Not at all sir" The detective said. "We are here to answer to the public, if and when we can do so and in your case we are grateful for your help". Gerald answered with a smile saying "Thank you". The two officers who had been sent ahead were walking quickly toward them. The detective moved in front of Gerald to see what they had found. He held his hand out to stop him coming closer whilst he spoke with the men. It was easy for Gerald to see as the shock on the detectives face told its own tale. "Sir" He said in a tone of authority. "You will have to wait here as beyond this point it could be a crime scene. I am sorry sir" He continued. "But the officers have found something which seems to be serious and needs further investigation. If you wait here sir an officer will take you back to the station." He walked off without another word. "That's all the thanks I get". Thought Gerald and he didn't have anything to tell the mother about Ann on his return. A young officer approached him and saluted saying

"Excuse me Sir, I have been asked to escort you back to the station, the car is on the far side of the house". He pointed to Gerald's boots and said "You will be pleased not to be walking in those fields again it will be more comftable in the car and in an hour or so we can be back in the station". Gerald smiled at him and answered with a nod of his head following him and getting into the passenger seat. The officer informed the detective on the phone that they were about to leave and the car slowly moved out from the crime scene.

The detective and his men were examining the floor, which was still soaked with the strong smell of bleach. "Rope this off" He shouted abruptly. "We shall need this area closed until forensics get here". They moved further into the house and some of the rooms were messy, especially where it looked as though heavy drinking sessions had been on the agenda. Cans littered the floor and the stench of stale beer and smoke was in the air, other than that there was nothing suspicious to see and it wasn't illegal to smoke weed on their own premises as long as they didn't sell it. "Don't let anyone into this area" The detective said to his colleague. "Our most important thing to do" He continued. "Is find the said bathroom which I presume is upstairs. You and I can find the one where she supposedly died and as there is no evidence as yet to that fact we can only look but I don't believe this is a wild goose trail". The two of them started up the stairs when the detective's phone rang. "I think you ought to see this Sir" The caller sounded urgent. "I'll be with you in a second" The detective answered the phone call. "We need to go now to the stables" The detective said turning and walking back down the stairs. "What about the bathroom, shall I continue?" His colleague asked. "No" was the answer. "We can search that later". They went quickly through the house and out to the stables. Four or five of the officers were standing at the stable doors when their guvnor arrived. "The look on your faces tells me there's got to be a body in there and as you all appear to be traumatised you had all better go and find some other work to do". He took a step into the stable saying. "It's not a bloody holiday camp." Two horses stood silently in the stable and all seemed fine except for a broken stall. "It had to be a kick from one of them to smash it." Muttered the detective and that's when he saw him. "What a mess." He declared. "Someone's covered him with straw and it's full of blood. I'm positive the horses didn't leave their stalls and cover the geezer to hide him, so until the missing girl is found this is our murder". Ann was glad they had found him, she was not sorry for the man but all the commotion was upsetting the horses and they are such sensitive creatures. He had looked after them well and they had liked him and now he was dead so who was going to feed them now. She went to pat them and they sheered up. "Horses are spooked" The detective's colleague said. "I'm not surprised" The detective answered. "Poor things have seen a lot". He took out his hanky and wiped his brow this place was making him sweat, clearing his throat he spoke to an officer close by. "You can ring the station and tell them to send a horse van to pick them up? We can let them run loose in the field until they come". Ann followed the horses as they were led out to a closure and left to run free, how she would have loved to ride them, not that she had ridden a horse before and I suppose now she never would. She watched them play for some time and began thinking about her mother and the way they used to play together when she was younger, she listened to her then. Ann needed her mother to find her before she could move on, she knew there was a special resting place to go to, but she wasn't ready yet. The sound from an Ambulance siren broke into her thoughts and she could see them arriving at the house. More police arrived with them and began putting on white overalls before entering the stables. Ann didn't need to see anymore she may as well travel back to see how Cindy and her mother were. She should find some comfort in seeing the two of them and she and Cindy may possibly connect again.

Ann appeared at the station almost immediately, one second she was outside of the house and the next in the entrance of the police station. It was a hive of activity they were bringing in a prisoner in handcuffs and Ann knew who it was. He was injured but could still walk and the fear in his face pleased Ann. She felt she could smile again knowing the police would question him and eventually find her. Cindy was sitting closely beside Ann's mother when an officer told them they were charging a man who had previously been at the house. He couldn't tell them any more at present but he would keep them informed, both of them started to cry. Ann wanted to hug her mother and tell her she was fine, as she wasn't hurting anymore. What a selfish person she had been to her mother. She loved her so very much and it was all her fault.. Ann knew the love was mutual and if she had done as her mother said there would have been no trouble. Cindy was still having tears and Ann's mother hugged her and offered her tissues to dry her eyes. "Thank you" Cindy said and Ann's mother shrugged her shoulders saying "Don't cry anymore they are going to find her". Cindy smiled a weak smile in her direction "I think we need some fresh air, just a little walk outside away from this place". "I believe you could be right" Was the reply. "Let's go". Holding hands, Ann watched them leave the room and she followed. The desk clerk looked up as they walked past, he nodded his head in recognition. A woman was sat in a corner looking as though she was waiting for someone to come out from one of the doors. "Can I speak to you two?" she shouted across to them. Ann's mother and Cindy were puzzled and the desk clerk asked the woman to be quiet and not to interfere with visitors to the station, meaning them. She beckoned to them with her fingers and mouthing words for them to go over to her. "Wonder what she wants?" Cindy said. "Shall we see?" They both walked toward her and the desk clerk said. "Talk with her if you want to but I can tell you now she is full of rubbish, we know her well. We bring her in for one thing or another most days". He laughed sarcastically and put his head down into his work again. Cindy thought the woman could be a Gypsy as she had a certain look about her. She had known a few as their camp was close by the big house and no matter how many times they were thrown off the campsite they came rolling back the next week. "Hello" Ann's mother said holding out her hand to shake. "I want to tell you something without those stupid coppers butting in". The woman pulled her closer and whispered in her ear. "Your daughter" She said "Is standing behind you". Ann's mother jumped back alarmed, this woman was playing with her head. "How dare you say such dreadful things, my daughter has been murdered". She wanted to hit the woman. "I knows you don't believe me". The woman continued. "She's a pretty girl with a beautiful smile, she's as big as me with long black wavy hair and she tells me it's hard to straighten and curls when it's rainy". The woman took a breath before adding. "She should have gone to school not the park". Cindy stepped in "You ought to be ashamed saying these things and upsetting people. You have no idea what this lady is going through and the police man should lock you up". Cindy was interrupted by the woman's reply. "I think they are going to dearie but she's still standing behind her mother". Ann's mother turned around thinking maybe she was there, Cindy took her hand and squeezed it saying to the woman. "The officer said you spoke lots of rubbish and we should have listened to him not you". Cindy put her arms around Ann's mother to comfort her and said "Ann was a blonde so you were wrong". "No, she is right, Ann had long black hair". Ann's mother was looking behind her still trying to see what the woman had seen. The officer behind the desk called the woman to come over to him, she got up and spoke to the two of them. "I know they are going to keep me here and I don't mind because what I did was stupid ". Cindy asked her "What did you do?" The woman grinned. "You're a bit nosy". She said. "But I'll tell you, I got caught". And laughed at her own joke. Taking Ann's mothers hand she gave her a card and curled her fingers over it. "Go there dearie you will be able to connect to your daughter, don't be afraid spirits will not harm you. Tell them Sally sent you, go soon your daughter is waiting for you". Before Ann's mother could answer, a door opened and Sally was ushered through it. The card bore the name of a Spiritualist Church and it appeared to be in the same vicinity as the police station. Cindy looked at the card puzzled. "Do you want to go there?" she said "Because if you do I want to come with you, although the idea of ghosts in those places have always scared me". "Yes! I really do want to" replied Ann's mother. "If there is the slightest chance of finding my little girl then I have to go. I miss her and love her and I know neither of us will be able to rest until she is found and I will try anything". The officer behind the desk glanced at them as they passed by. "We are going out for a bit of fresh air". Ann's mother called back softly. "We could be gone for an hour or so as we need a good walk". He nodded his approval saying he would tell his superiors where we had gone. Arm in arm they moved through the station doors. Cindy felt apprehensive regarding where they were going but Ann's mother could only think about seeing her daughter.

The Church was quite easy to find they only asked for directions twice and there it was. It appeared closed as the front gates were locked but there were steps going down to a basement and they could see a light, so someone was down there. Cindy hung behind while Ann's mother went down and rang the doorbell. The door opened and the face of a friendly young man looked out at them. "Can I help you"? He smiled warmly. "I hope so". Her mother answered. "I was told to say that Sally recommended the church and said we should pay you a visit". The young man looked up at Cindy. "Please come down" He said. "You are both welcome". Cindy felt a shiver go up and down her spine, his deep velvet voice was music to her ears. The apprehension she had felt before had melted away as the young man helped her down the last steps. He was tall and slim with a mischievous glint in his eye and Cindy felt a big attraction to him which surprised her. "Is this the first time you have been to a Spiritualist Church?" He asked and they both nodded. He continued saying. "We shall be opening the church soon for a service and tonight we have a medium who is excellent. All of our mediums are good but I especially like the one tonight who is also a personal friend of Sally". Cindy was listening and soaking in the sound of his dulcet tones. Ann's mother interrupted saying. "I have recently had a bereavement and lost my daughter, this is the reason we are here" she paused to brush away a tear from her face. "I wouldn't like you to get any false illusions" The man said. "We cannot say who will get a message through the medium". He smiled at Ann's mother saying. "If you are meant to receive a message from spirit they will know you are here". Cindy wanted to ask him about ghosts, as she didn't want to be frightened. She may be ignorant regarding spiritualists and their church but after Ann had died she had seen signs and could feel her around. "Will we see any one?" Cindy asked him. "If you mean any person who has passed to spirit then the answer is no, the only contact is the voice of the medium". Ann's mother was anxious to go into the church. "Do you think we could go upstairs?" "Of cause". He replied. "If you will both follow me, I shall have to open the doors now as service starts in another thirty minutes". They were close on his heels as they climbed another lot of steps up to the entrance of the church. The young man opened the door allowing Cindy and Ann's mother to enter. "What a lovely little church this is". Declared the mother of Ann. "I am pleased you like it" The young man answered "We too find it a lovely peaceful church and it brings to us a gentle faith that tells us life beyond death is eternal". He stopped speaking as he could see Cindy's face looking puzzled, had he gone too far? "Sorry" He said. "Sometimes

I can get carried away and I haven't introduced myself to you yet". Holding out his hand he shook hands with them both saying "My name is Derek, I am a committee member and a healer and we are happy that you came to see us. You can sit anywhere you like and if the medium comes to you just let them hear your voice". He handed them a hymn book and a glass of water. "I have to leave you as others are coming in for the service. Don't worry. He said to Cindy "There are no ghosts here that will frighten you". They found a pew four rows back from the podium where a table and two chairs stood, waiting to be occupied. The pews filled quickly while soft music played in the background and onto the podium stepped the church secretary accompanied with the lady medium who was introduced to all. Another few words from the secretary, including prayers for the sick and afterwards a song which everyone sang with gusto. Another prayer and one from the medium before she could begin to feel what the spirits wanted to say and who they wanted to contact. Her eyes wandered around searching each and every pew and alighted on a young couple in a corner. "May I speak with you?" She asked them. The girl nodded. "Could you answer me please as spirits can't hear nods, they need to hear your voice"? The girl answered with a "Yes". And the medium continued. "I feel I have a lady here who informs me that she liked to knit especially cardigans and she is laughing because you had to wear them and she knew you didn't want to. I feel this message is for your friend". The medium pointed to the girl's boyfriend sitting beside her. "Can you take the message?" she asked. The boy spoke out clearly. "I think it is my Grandmother every Christmas she gave me a cardigan and the last one she knitted for me could have been meant for Joseph, it was multi coloured". The medium laughed. "Your grandmother is full of fun and says you always took life too seriously and that was why she liked knitting cardigans. Take her love with you for she says you are always with her and God Bless". She was looking for another person to speak to when she stopped beside Cindy. "Someone in spirit wants to contact you but for some reason is being held back". The medium hesitated as if listening to someone then continued saying "I am informed by one of the relatives that the spirit concerned has not been there very long and is still in transit. Therefore they are not able to speak through me tonight. I am speaking of a young soul who was quite recently deceased. I believe it is the spirit of a girl and she is being well looked after, her relatives are sending a bouquet of flowers but they are not for you". The medium turned to look at Ann's mother and said. "The flowers are for you with love and I'll say thank you and. God bless". Cindy placed her arm around Ann's mother to comfort her. The young man Derek offered paper hankies as they both now were failing to hold back the tears. Sally had been right to send them here and Ann's mother knew she would have to return as tonight Ann had found a way of giving her flowers filled with love and it felt as though Ann had touched her. The church service was eventually over, some of the people went downstairs for refreshments. Ann's mother made her excuses and said what a good evening it had been. She didn't want to tell them why they needed to leave but they had to get back. Saying their goodbyes for now and promising to attend the church again, Cindy and Ann's mother walked hand in hand back toward the police station. It had been an evening full of events which the two of them had never expected. To have received a message from beyond the grave was unbelievable. How was it possible for one person to be able to talk to another on the other side of life? Ann's mother was puzzled but held on tight to the message and the flowers she had been given, she felt her daughter to be much closer to her now. Cindy knew her friend was wanting to tell them something and she would return to this church again and maybe find out what? She had to see that young man Derek again he was so nice. It had been a long time since she had fancied any fella.

Gerald Bourne was pacing outside of the station and waved before walking down the steps to greet them. "I wanted to tell you some good news and the desk sergeant told me you had gone out for a while. Come inside and I can tell you what I have been told". He seemed very excited as he ushered them into the room they had previously occupied. The two ladies sat on the large leather sofa in the corner and Gerald got plastic cups filled with tea for them from the machine. "You did ask for sugar?" He asked Cindy. She didn't answer, just nodded her head. "What have you got to tell us?" Ann's mother queried, taking the cup of tea she was offered. Gerald sat opposite them on a stool, clearing his throat he said. "I will come straight to the point, the police believe they know the whereabouts of your daughter and it is only a matter of time before she is found". Ann's mother couldn't believe what she was hearing. "Where is she, when will they bring her to me I must know where she is?" Graham got off the stool and went over to her. "They are going to explain everything to you later but they still have to ask further questions and more investigations, the man they have in custody is not yet charged". He was sorry that he didn't have more to tell her he could see how hurt she was. Gerald wanted to comfort her, under different circumstances he may have. She was a very beautiful woman even in grief her beauty shone through. "I don't know anymore but I was asked to explain things to you on your return". Cindy asked him if they had gone to look for Ann. "I believe so" Gerald answered and Ann's mother held out her hand for him to take and he kissed it gently. He had immense admiration for the lady. "You both have been booked into the George Hotel on the corner for the night as there will not be any further proceedings until tomorrow. I meanwhile have to go about my business but I am not about to desert you and will also be back here tomorrow, I wish you both a good night until we meet again in the morning". Gerald smiled as he went to leave the room, Ann's mother smiled back at him as he left. It was the first time she was able to and in her heart she knew she would find her daughter. She was feeling tired now and when Cindy said "Let's go to the hotel" she got up and followed her. The hotel was small owned by an elderly couple who kept it immaculate. They were greeted like old friends before being shown to their rooms. "Coffee and sandwiches will be sent up after you have time to settle in". The owner's wife said, leaving the two of them to do just that. Ann's mother threw her jacket off and kicked off her shoes and lay down on the bed, how tired she felt, she lay there thinking of Ann. Her mind wandered back to when she was small and very giggly and how she loved to stand on her head and do those somersaults and cartwheels. In her mind's eye she could see her standing before her and she went to take her hand. A knock on the door brought her back to reality. "Room Service". A voice called. Opening her eyes Ann wasn't in the room, it was all in her imagination. She stood up and went to the door for the tray. "Thank you it is so kind of you to get this ready". The lady answered saying it was a pleasure and if they needed anything else they could ring downstairs. The police had booked the rooms in the hotel and the owners knew why they were staying with them and the reason for the older person's sadness, as for the younger girl they weren't sure how she fitted into the program. Ann knew her mother couldn't see her but she had almost made contact, she had felt the warmth of her hand. How different she was now, her mother was always self-assured in charge of everything and now she was more like a broken piece of crockery that couldn't be put back together again. Ann stayed with her even after she turned out the lights and fell into a deep sleep. It was a chance for her to cuddle up close and tell her how much she loved her for the rest of the night. Ann's mother dreamed about her lost daughter and hearing soft words whispered into her ears. It was the only comfort Ann could give and one she got in return. Morning came and with it the warm sunshine when Ann's mother awoke, for a moment she was happy and then ashamed for being so, she had no right to be happy again. Cindy too was awake and feeling better than she had been for a long time, she had needed that sleep. She took a shower and stayed under the water until her skin sizzled. Getting herself dressed Cindy went to knock for Ann's mother thinking they could go down for breakfast together. She knocked and waited then knocked again but there was no answer. "Maybe she already is down having breakfast". Cindy said to herself aloud. The dining room had a handful of people in there and not a sign of Ann's mother. The owner's wife came over to her. "Which table would you like?" She asked. "I am not sure yet". Cindy looked around before finishing her sentence "Have you seen my friend this morning?" "Yes" the lady answered her. "She came down earlier but she didn't want anything to eat". She paused before adding. "The lady insisted you have some breakfast and said to tell you she will be at the police station and will see you there after you have eaten". Cindy laughed and ordered something to eat and enjoyed every morsel. She was well refreshed after eating breakfast and before leaving the hotel said they could be back for another night. She thanked them saying "She would need to ask her friend first". She strolled out of the hotel crossed the road, climbing the steps into the police station.

It was a hive of activity in the station with police officers moving from one office to the next, opening doors and banging them closed again. Ann's mother was standing talking with Gerald in the far corner. He beckoned to Cindy to join them, she was going to anyway he didn't need to call her over. "Did you eat?" Ann's mother asked. "Yes I did and enjoyed it" Cindy replied. "The lady gave me your message" She continued. "I was very hungry". "I thought you would be" Ann's mother answered. "Ann was the same always hungry, I didn't want anything". She broke down crying and Gerald put his arm around her for comfort. "Sorry" she said. "I promised myself not to cry again until Ann was found but the police have found a body and can't tell me anymore until they have proof of identity". There was a lot of commotion going on outside and the police were bringing in a man and a woman, both wearing handcuffs. The Paparazzi had gathered too they were after a story, they had found out something important was a foot and they were intent on finding out what it was. Shouting, followed by flash bulbs and the Television people were there too. "Are we able to go back to the small room away from this noise, where we were before?" Cindy asked Ann's mother. "We shall have to ask them" She answered her. "They are so busy this morning and I wonder who those two people are they have arrested, could they have anything to do with my Ann? While they were talking Gerald asked the desk clerk if they could use the room again. "It's there to accommodate you all sir" Was the answer. Gerald looked at Cindy and she seemed so much better after a nights rest and food. Ann's mother wasn't doing so well, she needed help and if she would allow him he would be there for her. "It's ok to use the room as long as we need it and the machine is there for a cup of tea". He said and went to hold the door to the room open. Gerald waited until Cindy and Ann's mother joined him, closing the door behind them. "It'll be good to get away from all that noise". Gerald said offering Ann's mother a cushion for her back as she sat on a two seated couch. Cindy got three teas and sat in an armchair leaving Gerald the choice of the couch with Anns mother or a hard chair that was tucked under a small table. There was a window seat which looked out onto the front of the station but sitting there might encourage the paparazzi to use their cameras, he decided on the table chair. He would have loved to be close to Ann's mother to comfort her but it could prove to be wrong as she wasn't thinking the same as he was and it was only a small couch where closeness couldn't be avoided. A breeze blew the curtains and it chilled the room quickly. "This is a darned cold room". Gerald shivered. Cindy turned to the radiators feeling for any heat in them. "They are hot" She said "It's very strange" Cindy was cuddling the cushion for warmth. Ann's mother smiled, "We have a visitor here and I can feel it's my daughter, I have no idea why I believe this but I can almost smell her". She stood up closing her eyes and breathed in deeply. "In my mind's eye she is standing before me and if I reach out I can touch her". Cindy and Gerald looked puzzled at one another. "Come and sit down for a while" Gerald said taking her arm. He was shaken off and Ann's mother sounded annoyed saying "You don't have to believe it but I do". The curtains started blowing again and this time wildly as if there was a hurricane on the way. Both Cindy and Gerald were struck dumb there was definitely someone or something in the room that wasn't entirely human. Ann didn't want to scare anyone she wanted them to know that she was here and could hear their words and thoughts. She also knew how much they cared. She was here as her mother needed to feel her love too. Ann herself was as happy as a spirit could be, the two odious people from the first farm had been caught. The other man they had under arrest had told the police where they could be found. He had decided if he had to go down they would come with him, he wasn't going to do time alone. Ann had enjoyed being present during the investigation and joining in with the arrests. It gave her immense pleasure watching the fear materialize on their faces as they were led down to the holding cells. She would have loved to put some extra fear into them but it wasn't easy and she needed her strength to stay in contact with her mother and friend. Maybe they will go back to that Spiritualist church again, it was easier with a medium she could help in making contact with the living. She decided to go there for a visit because if any other spirits were like her this beautiful church is where she would find them and right now she needed friends. How right she was, it was amazing. Golden Orbs' circled around to greet her omitting soft sighs when they moved. Ann knew these spirits welcomed her and for a while she was at peace.

Crowds were gathering outside of the police station, they had to be moved away from the entrance as they were hindering the police work. Ann's mother and Cindy were wondering why so many people were outside. Gerald acted as a spokesman for them. "Excuse me" Gerald said to an Inspector. "Could you tell us what is happening?" The Inspector ushered him into an office and sat him down opposite the desk. "We haven't identified the body yet, we are still waiting for dental x rays and then we should know. As for the crowds outside there has been a leek and once the press smell a story there is no way we can stop them. I can tell you this, which is not for the ears of the press. We have learned from the accused that this is not the first time young girls have been kidnapped by this gang. We have also been told that the buyers are from foreign lands, mostly the Middle East. They arrive in London wanting to spend their money and arrangements are made through a middle man who puts out his feelers to certain men who frequent parks and runaways in railway stations, I believe they are considered as easy prey." He said shaking his head and got up from the desk. "I cannot tell you much more yet sir except we are on our way to the airport where we are lying in wait to apprehend certain people as they pass through and another arrest is imminent, could be today or next week but eventually it will prove fruitful". Gerald thanked him for the information and also asked if there was another exit from the building. "Yes sir, let me show you the back way out of the station. You are wise sir to avoid the press, they can be a nuisance and very persuasive". They walked past the offices and through a canteen around the back of a kitchen to where there was a door marked emergency exit. "This is your way out but you cannot enter again this way, you will have to choose your moment when you are ready to return". The Inspector went to open the door and Gerald stopped him. "Not yet" He said. "I shall have to get the ladies as we need to return to the hotel tonight. I just wanted to know how we could go out without those crowds seeing us but thank you." Taking his hand from the door handle the Inspector answered Gerald. "Sorry sir my mistake, I thought you wanted to go out now. When you and the ladies want to go please inform the desk, safety first you know". They walked back through the canteen and past the offices, the Inspector turned and saluted, leaving Gerald there while he went about his duties. The ladies had the TV on when Gerald entered the room. Ann's mother was anxious to find out any news and was hoping the television would inform her as here in the station everything was hush, hush. "Hello ladies" Gerald said. "Sorry I have been a while but there is another way out where we won't be seen. So if you both are ready we can go back to the hotel and make sure there are rooms free for us tonight and from there we can have a good meal, not in the hotel as I have seen a good curry house further down the road." Cindy was on her feet quickly. "Brilliant" She answered him. "Let's go". Ann's mother switched the set off, picked up her bag and followed them out without saying a word. They went through the door at the rear of the kitchen with Gerald making sure he closed it behind them and out into the cool air. The crowds eyes were all glued to the front of the station and didn't see them leaving at the rear. Gerald gave a satisfied chuckle. "We made it" He said. "Follow me, the restaurant is only a short distance away and I've rang the hotel so there is no need to worry about that". He looked at Ann's mother seeing the sadness in her face and smiled gently at her saying. "Would you care to take my arm? It is good to be able to lean on someone when life is at its heaviest and I am pleased to be here for you, if you will let me?" I believe Ann's mother was grateful for the offer because she slid her hand through his arm as they walked toward the curry house. Cindy kept close behind them looking in shop windows, her eyes alighted on a red dress but seeing the price she felt disappointed. She didn't have any money that could buy it anyway and at that price one would have to be a millionaire. She had to run to catch up with them and tripped. "Are you alright?" A voice asked helping her to her feet. "Yes thank you, I am fine" She answered and laughed as she saw who it was. "I feel so silly now". She said. "Why do all things like that happen when we don't want to be seen?" He laughed back at her. "I am glad you did fall over, otherwise we might not have met again". He really did find her attractive. "Oh no Derek". Cindy answered him. "We were definitely coming to the church tonight but right now I need to catch up to my friends as we are all going for a meal". She hesitated before saying. "We haven't eaten all day and decided to have a curry, would you care to join us?" Derek shook his head. "I would love to eat with you some other time if I may but tonight I have to assist at the church, can we take a rain cheque on that?" He squeezed her hand and she reciprocated.

"Hope we see you later" Derek said as he walked away. "You will" she called back. "See yer". And hurried after the other two. Derek continued toward the church, there was much to do before the congregation arrived. His first job was making sure the church was warm, it could be cold if not heated properly and people complained if it was chilly. He made his way up to the organist's balcony, the organ wasn't played anymore but stood there regal and beautiful. A music system was used to play for the congregation now, it was easier with lots of favourite tunes and didn't need an expert to play it. Derek was busy sorting out the music for the evening, he was a true man of music and knew how it soothed the soul including his own as most of his life he had been writing it. A creak sounded and it made him jump, looking around he could see the place was empty but the turntable was moving and he hadn't switched it on yet. "I must have knocked it on accidently" He said aloud, switching it off again. A small breeze blew across his face with a slight shushing sound, Derek was feeling a little cold which was strange as the heating was adequate enough. From where he was standing Derek could see over the balcony into the body of the church below and a step up from there was the speakers rostrum. Circling around the rostrum appeared to be two spiritual orbs, he watched mesmerized. He had on occasions seen orbs before but only on photographs and he realized someone was trying to say they were here and needing to be heard. Although he couldn't see anyone Derek spoke aloud. "Thank you for letting me know of your presence and tonight the medium will help you to relay your message, God Bless you". He said as he felt the hairs standing up on his arms and he was shivering with the cold. Within minutes after saying God Bless a warm breeze caressed his face and the church started feeling warm again. His heart was beating fast when he climbed down the stairs, not with fright but excitement and anxious to tell what he had seen. After the service the congregation were welcome to go downstairs for a chat and a hot drink of tea or coffee. Two committee members had arrived and they were helping to make the tables ready. Mandy, a long standing member almost dropped one of the cups when Derek rushed into the room saying what he had seen. "Slow down a bit Derek". She said. "What's happened? You look like you've seen a ghost". Derek nodded his head before saying "I believe I almost have". "Wait a minute" Mandy said going to get her friend Janet and they both sat open mouthed waiting for Derek to get his breath and say what he had seen. They listened intently and when he had finished Janet said. "There was a strange light up there and it hovered in the corner last night, I wasn't scared because I thought it could have been a reflexion from a car light". Derek took a drink of water, his throat felt dry, he coughed and said "Someone is trying to tell us something and it must be important". Mandy answered him "I haven't seen or heard anything although it appears the spirits do want to communicate with someone. The medium is due at any time now and we don't want to feed her with any information, if they want to give a message she will feel their presence and direct the message to the person concerned". A knock on the door interrupted their conversation. "She has arrived, I'll let her in". And Janet went to open the door. "Don't say anything" Mandy called quietly. "It's between us three". They all greeted her to the church and she answered by saying. "It's a pleasure for me to be able to work here, it is a beautiful church and I pray tonight the messages that I receive will bring much love and light to all that are in the congregation". Derek smiled at her and made his excuses as he had to be there to welcome in the worshipers and collect their donations, which went toward the upkeep of the church. The pews were filling and Derek's mind tonight was of Cindy, would she come? It was almost time for the service to begin and he climbed the stair up to the balcony and placed the disc on the player. The gentle music sifted through and leaning over for one last look at the gathering his heart missed a beat, she was there. Lifting up her head toward the music their eyes met and for the first time in her life Cindy blushed. Ann's mother was close behind her and saw the look, it was one she well remembered and she was pleased for them. Gerald followed them in paying the donations and sat down beside Ann's mother. He held out his hand to her and she took hold of it, she felt and knew tonight she would need a strong hand to hold her. Ann wanted her in the church, her scent was everywhere. The service began and singing filled the air, prayers followed with kind words for the sick then all fell silent as the medium took the rostrum ready to converse with spirit. She had a message for the lady on the front row and one for a young man, his grandfather said he had his watch and not to keep winding it so hard. The young man laughed and said "Yes I do have his watch". The medium moved on to a couple and then to an elderly lady on the back pew, a tissue was needed for her tears. "I do have another message here which comes with a big bouquet of roses and they wish to say sorry". She moved over to the other side of the rostrum and appeared to be talking to an invisible person. "I am told to say they are well and being looked after by friends and relatives. Also I am feeling a sense of torment mixed with sorrow because of your unhappiness... I feel that I have to come in that direction". Her eyes alighted onto Ann's mother. "Can you take this message?" She asked. "Yes I think so". She answered. "Your daughter, I am told has recently passed to spirit and she is here now. As a matter of fact she is standing behind you and smiling, in her hands she is holding the roses as a gift for you". It was Ann's mother who needed tissue now and Gerald was there for a shoulder to cry on. The medium continued saying. "She doesn't want you to cry or be sad anymore as one day she says, we will meet again. She also tells me there is another person waiting to enter your life who will be understanding and good for you. I can't tell you anything else". The medium said "The young lady has gone, thank you and god bless". She turned and began speaking to another person in the centre pew. Gerald was standing ready with another tissue as Ann's mother leaned in on him for support. Derek asked Cindy if she knew the girl who was in spirit, he didn't need an answer just the box of tissues. The service was almost over and Derek would be able to speak more with her then. From the moment he first saw her he knew she was troubled and he wanted to hold her and tell her he would protect her. Protect her from what? He had no idea what their trouble was but someone had been trying to tell him earlier. He had been given the gift of a Healer and if she allowed him twenty minutes, with the help of God he may be able to help her. His thoughts were broken into by the Mediums prayer then a goodnight and God bless, one by one the congregation trouped out. "Will you be going downstairs for refreshments?"

Derek asked Cindy. "Maybe" she replied. "If the other two are then I will". When they went downstairs Derek was pleased now he would be able to find out what it was that troubled her so. Gerald led Ann's mother over to a table in the corner picking up cups of tea from the bar on the way, he too wanted to know more but especially about her. The look he gave to Derek had a meaning behind it, he wanted to be alone with her. Derek realized and Cindy found herself being taken to a table at the back of the room. Glancing over to where the other two were sitting she too could tell Gerald wanted time alone with Ann's mother. Cindy had known for a good while that Gerald was besotted with her. Derek decided to come straight to the point with Cindy. "You were in tears when the medium spoke to your friend, were the words she spoke about her daughter?" He paused before saying "Could this have been the young girl who has been missing from home and believed dead?" Cindy answered him quietly with a "Yes". Derek covered her hands with his before asking. "Did you know her?" Cindy began to tell him how they met and the reasons they were both in the house. They had big plans for her and being so young she was very sellable. Dark looking foreign men had offered a great deal of money for her and with her hair dyed blonde it excited them. The boss at the house demanded double of what they had offered and they refused to pay before trying the goods". She stopped talking to wipe away a tear and Derek squeezed her hands to reassure her. She continued saying. "Ann seemed to know what was happening and while she was getting ready in a bath of sweet smelling suds she asked me to leave the room which I did, I presumed she needed her privacy". "What happened?" Derek interrupted her. Cindy let the tears flow and hung on tightly to Derek's shoulder. "She drowned herself before they could do any more to her, she was a beautiful person and didn't deserve being treated like an old prostitute". She hesitated before continuing. "I want to tell you, no; I need to let you know the truth, prostitute was my label when I went there". Derek took her hands in his again, he didn't care what she had been before they met and for her to trust him with her secret made him feel so special and honoured. "I wasn't kidnapped like Ann". She said. "I was older and knew what I was getting into, all I was interested in was the money. That is not me anymore, they took a young girl and treated her disgustingly. I found out later this had been done many times before and I was shocked and ashamed to be part of it. I want you to believe me I am a changed person now and until the whole of the gang are caught I shall not rest". "Things will take time to get better". Derek said softly. "And if you need me I will be there for you". He was smitten, it had been a number of years since he had last felt this way about anyone. Cindy felt at ease with him and asked to be walked to the hotel. Gerald said they were just finishing their refreshments and would follow them in five minutes. Cindy and Derek left the church still holding hands. At the entrance to the hotel they said their goodbyes with a passionate kiss and Derek felt he needed more as he was trembling. Cindy was used to these passions from men but he was different and it wasn't fair to him to linger, so she just said goodnight and went in through the entrance. "I will call for you tomorrow" He called and she waved back. The Spirit Orbs in the church knew this would happen and tonight he would say a special thank you for their help. There was no passionate kiss between Ann's mother and Gerald but a simple caress of hands touching and as they reached their hotel he kissed her on both cheeks then taking her hand he bent and kissed it before walking away to his room. Ann was delighted as she watched knowing her mother was about to discover a new love and her friend Cindy would begin to have a new life, far away from the old sordid one. She wanted to hug them but knew it was impossible, up in the church she felt really close especially with the young man whom she knew had seen her frolicking with her spirit friends. It had been good fun dancing to his music, he had seen them and wasn't scared and it allowed her to connect with the medium easily. He would be a good partner for Cindy, neither of them knew this yet but she did and it gave her some satisfaction knowing that happiness lay ahead not only for Cindy but her mother too.

Sleep was needed and Ann's mother was more relaxed than she had been for a long time. She said her goodnight to Ann telling her how much she missed and loved her, closed her eyes and was soon fast asleep. Cindy lay there thinking about Derek and his deep sexy voice, she too closed her eyes and he was still there in her dreams. Gerald couldn't sleep he kept mulling over all he had been told and feeling a great sadness for the lovely lady, she was so brave. He still didn't know her first name which was strange but for some reason he had never asked and he hadn't heard anyone using it. Tomorrow morning he would ask her name as he wanted to really get to know her and care for her. Something had happened which he couldn't explain and he hoped she felt it too, with the passing of time maybe she would. Morning came around quickly and Cindy awoke feeling refreshed although she felt a little sorry knowing her dream was just that. In last nights dream she and Derek were making love as soon as her head hit the pillow. A knock on the door and it was Ann's mother saying she was going down to breakfast. Cindy replied with an "OK I'll be another ten minutes, I will see you down there". Gerald was already sitting at the table waiting for the ladies to join him and when Ann's mother entered the breakfast room he stood up to greet her. A kiss to her cheek and then pulling the chair out for her to sit on. "Did you sleep well?" He asked her. She smiled saying "It was the first time I have been able to sleep a full night for weeks and I believe it was because my daughter gave a message and I could feel her close to me". "Would you go there again?" Gerald queried. "Of cause I will" She said indignantly. "If it was your daughter you would go there too". She patted his hand and said. "Sorry; that was a little bit too sharp, I didn't mean it to sound that way". "You have every reason to think and feel as you do" Gerald answered. "I would never take offence whatever you say to me, you have been through too much and I admire the way you handle things". Cindy arrived saying she was starving and could we order? Which they did straight away and breakfast was good. It was only a small hotel but was definitely first class. Ann's mother said to Cindy. "We will have to go over to the police station after we have eaten it is possible they may have more to tell us about Ann". Gerald interrupted her saying. "Your daughter had a sweet name but I have been trying to learn yours, I find it almost impossible to address you I either say excuse me, or ask you a question just to get your attention. Now I am introducing myself to you, my name is Gerald Bourne and you are?" This time she really laughed and catching her breath she spoke back to him. "All this time you didn't know, you are so funny". He wanted her to laugh but not at him. "Seriously" He said. "Would you please tell me your name"? "My name Sir is Victoria Hammond and you may call me Vicky". They shook hands and Gerald said "I am very pleased to meet you Vicky". And they both found it highly amusing.

Derek had thought about Cindy late into the night and what she had told him about herself. He would eventually have got to know from newspaper reports as they can dig deeply into people's past. She didn't have to tell him, the fact is she did and his admiration of her had soared. It was dreadful that the young girl died and must have been very frightening for Cindy seeing her there, she was one brave female. His thoughts turned back to the church and the Orbs he had seen so clearly and afterwards the messages given to the medium. Spirits are not revengeful, they have only a certain amount of time to spend on the earthly plane in which to help rectify situations of this calibre. Derek could feel this was why their presence was around the church, so her mother was right it must have been a message from her daughter. He was outside of the police station now and so was the Paparazzi. Nine thirty in the morning, they must have been here all night waiting for news to break. There was no sign of Cindy or the other two, she had mentioned an exit in the back door if he could push through this lot he would be able to make his way to the rear of the building. Moving past a couple of photographers one turned and a flash went off in his face. "Why did you take a photo of me?" Derek wanted to know. "Sorry mate" was the answer "I am taking pictures of everybody and I may get lucky, who knows you could be the geezer they are looking for". Derek had to smile, they were only doing their job. He walked around to the back of the police station and sat up on a waste bin, it was early and he could wait. He had been there an hour and wondered if they were already inside and he could possibly have missed them, jumping down from the bin he landed with his knees bent and when he lifted up his head Cindy was in front of him, Gerald was following with Ann's mother. "Good morning" Cindy said. "Have you been waiting long?" "No" Derek answered her. "Maybe ten minutes or so". He wasn't going to admit to being there longer. "Stay with us" Gerald said to him. "They will allow you inside if you want to, it's up to you". Cindy interrupted him with "Of cause he wants to join us" and held out her hand to Derek and he didn't hesitate but took hold eagerly. Ann's mother, Vicky went in first then Gerald who held the door open for Cindy and Derek. They immediately went to their allotted room and kept the blinds closed keeping unwanted eyes out. The police inspector in charge of the case was accompanied with two other officers, one being a woman and together they entered the room. "A good morning, to you all and I hope you are feeling a little better today". The Inspector went over to Derek saying "Could you tell me why you are here this morning sir?" Before Derek could answer Cindy answered for him. "He is my boyfriend and he is keeping me company, we have missed each other so much". The Inspector apologised saying they had to know who was in the station as inquiries were still in progress and not for public knowledge yet. "We do have some news for you" He said, pointing to Ann's mother. "The lady officer is here to assist you with any queries you may have and she will inform you of any further investigations we are pursuing, I will leave you now in her capable hands as I have more information to follow up. Thank you for your attention and we may meet later with more news". He left the room with the other officer, leaving the female officer to talk with them. "If you can all be seated" The police woman said. "There is something I would like to say to Mrs Hammond of a delicate matter". She sat beside Ann's mother on the sofa touching her arm. "We have done a great deal of work in finding out if the dental impressions were a match of your daughter's teeth, we are now positive that they did belong to your missing daughter". Gerald was sat at the other side of her and he took her into his arms for comfort. Cindy brought her a cup of tea and then moved away to the back of the room with Derek. Vicky took a sip of the tea, she wasn't going to cry. She looked at Gerald and smiled saying. "I am Ann's mother and I know she is not being hurt anymore. I will not shed another tear until the day they find the leaders of this disgusting gang. My daughter cannot rest in peace until they are made to pay for what has happened to her". The police woman stood up, she was relieved it had gone so well. "You can be assured Mrs Hammond". She said. "Eventually they will be apprehended, the airports are being closely watched and we also have information which could be a strong lead. I would like to tell you more but at this moment there is nothing else I can, except to say that I am sorry to be the bearer of this sad news". Vicky got up from the sofa and held out her hand to the officer and they shook hands. "Thank you for telling me, it couldn't have been an easy thing to do but I do appreciate everything you all are doing". The female officer had undergone training to deal with things like this but no amount of training could give her the strength which this woman possessed. She needed to get out of this room and back to the safety of the office before she disclosed her weakness in front of them, she was close to tears. "I will be back later, maybe have a spot of lunch in the canteen together". "We'd love to". Gerald called out as she left the room whilst reaching to hold onto Vicky's hand. Cindy and Derek had decided to go back to the church and they were about to tell the other two of their decision, even a fool could tell they needed to be alone. "Are you alright" Cindy asked Ann's mother. She answered her in a quiet voice. "Don't worry Cindy I am fine and with time I shall be much better. I am very lucky to have you, my daughter's friend and Gerald to lean on". She turned to Derek saying "Sorry I meant you too. It was because of you my daughter's spirit came to me and for this I will be eternally grateful". Cindy interrupted her to say. "Derek and I are going to the church, and if you both feel you want to join us later in a prayer, please come". Gerald replied to Cindy. "We will be there, all we want at this moment is to hear more of the investigations. Give us another hour or so and we should be across there." Gerald was already speaking for Vicky and she felt a support she so badly needed.

It was still early, the church smelt musty and it would be two hours before the service started. Derek had the keys for the door, he could also open a window or two for fresh air and Cindy and he could talk inside. On entering the building he looked upward to the balcony wondering if the spirits were there watching him, maybe they were and laughing. "Penny for your thoughts" Cindy said, pushing him gently. "Do you think Ann is here?" She asked. "I am not a medium, so I'm not able to answer that question but I can feel something that is making my heart jump". He smiled at Cindy and continued with. "My heart tells me this is nothing to do with spirit and only you can calm the beat". Cindy thought he was joking and reacted with a tender back slap. Turning around he took her into his arms and kissed her passionately, even if it was a surprise she reciprocated. Remembering he was in a church brought Derek to an immediate stop, which left Cindy blushing. Ann was standing right beside them and she too blushed, feeling like a Peeping Tom. If only they could see her what a surprise they would have. Ann was wanting to have a bit of fun with the two of them but the other spirits had said it was wrong and she shouldn't interfere in that way. Cindy sat down on a pew and Derek placed his hand on her shoulder. "I am not sorry" He said "I have wanted to kiss you from the first time we met but I was afraid you would object and I would lose the chance of telling you how I feel." He sat down beside her, holding both of her hands and looking into her eyes. Cindy answered saying. "I didn't expect you to kiss me like you did". She hesitated, and Derek wondered if he had been wrong and he should apologise now. "I wanted you to kiss me" She said. "I think it was the sound of your voice that I first liked and then I got attracted to the whole package." They hugged and laughed together. Ann was pleased knowing they had found each other and she desperately wanted to tell them. The song books for the sermon were piled on the side desk, waiting for the congregation to take them and Ann decided this was how she would tell them. The pages of the song books began turning fast which astonished Derek, and Cindy was shaking. "Don't be afraid"

He held her tightly. "Someone is trying to tell us something". The pages stopped turning and Derek went to see where they had finished, Cindy followed him. The page was laying open on a love song and on the page was placed a button. Picking up the button Cindy began to shed a tear. "Ann was here and maybe still is, this is a message from her and I am so pleased she has been able to say she is happy for us". She kissed the button before saying. "Thank you Ann, and may God Bless you". The congregation were arriving and finding their seats for the service. Derek was up on the balcony sorting out the music when Vicky with Gerald entered sitting beside Cindy. They acknowledged each other and the music started, the sound of singing filled the air. The medium was up on the Rostrum and when the singing was over led the congregation into prayers, afterwards she gave messages from spirit. She had only a small message for Vicky which was. "I am with Granny and she says to tell you that snuggles is here and he's still a naughty dog". Ann's mother couldn't believe what she was hearing, she did have such a dog when she was young and only her own mother could have told Ann this. She knew her daughter's spirit would never be far away from her even if her body had left the earthly plain. She bowed her head remembering her voice, face and her lovely hair and said a silent prayer with her eyes closed. Gerald said nothing, this time was hers to cherish. Upstairs on the balcony Derek felt a presence, he couldn't see anything but he knew he wasn't alone, as the hairs stood up on his arms and there was an intense coldness around him. While the congregation were singing their final hymn to Derek's music, he was visited by Ann. She stood before him like a ray of sunshine with her thick long hair blowing across her face. He was amazed that he could see her so clearly and honoured to think she had chosen him to show her image to. Ann was gone as quickly as she appeared, leaving behind a picture in Derek's mind of seas and yachts. The coldness went along with the vision, but the thought in his mind lingered and he would have to discuss it with Cindy before telling the others. It had to be a message from Ann, why would he think about sea and yachts after seeing her? It had to be important and she had found this way of telling him. Maybe she had chosen him as he was always in the church and being alone upstairs made it easier for her to make a connection. The service was over and all were leaving, some went downstairs for refreshments and Cindy, Vicky and Gerald sat together waiting for Derek to join them. He was looking serious when he eventually came to sit down. "While you were all singing the last hymn" He said. "I was visited by a young lady on the balcony, she didn't say anything to me and she was only there for a fleeting moment. She did leave me with a strange thought in my head, which I cannot shake away". Ann's mother, Vicky was the first to speak. "It was my daughter, wasn't it?" Derek nodded his head in reply. "What message do you think you were you given?" Vicky continued. Derek answered her telling them about the yachts and the sea. "I think" He said. "We are to look for boats or yachts leaving this country, they would have to sign a contract of sorts to say they are clear to leave and the police should be able to get the information". "There is no evidence" Gerald interrupted Derek. "They are not going to believe you if you tell them it was a message from spirit, they will think it's all in your mind". Cindy was still holding the button and turning it over in her hand.

"What if I said, I heard them discussing going to sea". The button was becoming warm in her hands. "That's an idea worth following". Gerald said, turning to Vicky for her approval and she agreed. Derek was pleased, it had to be Ann's way of telling them where to find the men responsible for abducting young girls. They were on the South Coast so the probability was it was close by, but where? They had all decided what must be done and left the vicinity of the church making their way to the police station. Around the back of the crowds, who were still hanging about for news and photographs of the murdered girls family and in through the back entrance. Reaching their room each of them sat down and immediately started to discuss what they should tell the inspector. Ann's mother, Vicky was the first to speak. "We should let Cindy bring up of how she heard the men's conversation of going to sea, and she wondered if they might escape this way". There was a knock on the door and it opened. "Good evening to you all and I hope you have had a good afternoon". It was the lady officer who greeted them and they all smiled and nodded in reply. "I haven't any further news for you but the airports are under strict surveillance and their passports will be seen, so you have no need to worry about them getting away". They all looked at each other and Cindy stood up. "Do you think it is possible for me to see the Inspector who is in charge of the case?" The lady officer seemed puzzled but said. "Of cause you may, he will be pleased to see you. I hope it's not because we are upsetting you as we are here to help you all as much as we can". Cindy and Vicky answered with a "No" and Gerald said. "It isn't you or your officer friends upsetting us, it is just that Cindy remembered something that could be important to the case, so if she could see the Inspector soon he may be able to use what she knows." The relief and then the surprise on the lady officer's face showed clearly. "I'll go now" She said, leaving the room. Within a few minutes the phone rang and Gerald answered it. "It's for you Cindy, the Inspector is calling". He handed the phone over to Cindy, who almost tripped over her own feet to get it. "Hello, hello it's me Inspector, Cindy". She paused to get her breath before saying "I've got something to tell you that I had forgotten about and I think it may be important". The inspector interrupted her to say "I shall be with you all shortly and when you tell me what you have remembered I shall tell you what we have found out, and you could be surprised. I am only fifteen minutes away so I won't be long." Cindy was still speaking but the line was dead. The Inspector arrived at the station and called his officers into the main investigation room and together they discussed what was happening with the case. "I am about to talk with the young lady Cindy from the house, who believes she can give us some more information that she previously overlooked. They will be pleased about the arrest we made at the airport especially the victim's mother, now I will go to see them." He said, picking up his briefcase and leaving the investigations office. The visitors room went quiet when he entered, in anticipation of what was about to be said. "If you can all be seated I will be able to inform you of what has been happening with our investigations". Ann's mother and Cindy sat together on the sofa, Gerald sat on the arm and Derek straddled a chair. The Inspector continued. "You will be pleased to know that we apprehended the two foreign men at the airport, we were very lucky, seemingly the plane had been delayed due to some mechanical fault. During this time a call was made from one of their mobiles which was waylaid by security. A translator had to be called and there was enough evidence to make an arrest. Trafficking to and from these countries has long been known but we have not been able to prove it, perhaps now we will." He smiled and Ann's mother bit her lip, to stop the tears. Turning to Cindy he said. "I understand you have some information to tell me, is that true?" "Yes it is" Cindy answered him. "I overheard them speaking about taking the girls by sea on a yacht, which belongs to the big boss. We are close to the Isle of Weight and they have yachts over there". The Inspector was turning it over in his mind, she could be right, he thought. "We shall look into this straight away, there has to be someone of substantial means running this disgusting business of exploiting girls and drug running. Thanks to your memory young lady we may be able to get the instigator of this horrendous business".

Ann had been keeping an eye on all the goings on and even if she was becoming weaker she was still strong enough to follow them. "This was Portsmouth, she had been here with her mother last year". The policemen were getting into a small speed boat, she was glad she didn't need to. The sea was choppy and a couple of officers were not very happy and wishing they hadn't eaten that sausage roll. Ann was waiting for them when they reached the Isle of Weight and disembarked. If spirits can laugh, she did as they looked a sorry sight. The Harbour masters office stood close by and the policemen walked immediately over to it, up the steps and in. It was busy around the harbour as they were getting their yachts ready for the big race, which would be happening within the next week. The larger boats and yachts were preparing or leaving the area, the whole seafaring basin was a hive of activity. Ann moved away and out into the water toward an elegant yacht that floated there. It was gleaming white with shiny porthole windows, on deck beautiful sun lounges and a table baring succulent fruits. Glasses half filled with champagne lay idol as if waiting for someone to come and finish their drink. A sound of music blared out from below and Ann followed the rhythm. She could tell why they played their music so loud, the young girls who kept the ship clean during the day were by nightfall sex slaves to the owner and associates. The men sat cross legged on cushions, which spread out across the room. In front of them girls shimmied and belly danced their bare feet gracefully moving across the floor. As they passed by a man, his arm reached out pulling one of the girls down onto the cushion beside him and roars of laughter would break out. Ann had to look away as he began mauling the female, whose cries went unheard. The music played louder as one by one the other girls fell onto the cushions, each taking their turn in sharing their favours with the other men. A male servant entered carrying a tray of drinks with a small package on it and placed it on the table beside the owner. He told him to get out and waved him away, keeping a tight hold on his girl he emptied the contents of the package onto the tray. With the knife he always kept with him he divided the powder into long lines of cocaine. He dipped his finger into the powder and licked it, dipping in again he wiped it under the girls nose. She rubbed it off with her hands, she didn't want to be a junkie. This act of refusal annoyed him and taking her head he shoved it full into the powder and kept it there. Her face was squashed and her lungs were crying out for air, she had to breathe. Lifting her head slightly he said. "Now fill your lungs bitch". A deep snatch of air filled her chest along with the powder she had tried to resist, her head was spinning the world was turning upside down and now she felt she could do anything. He was on top of her and giving her more of that delicious powder to put up her nose, she was laughing and taking off her clothes, what did she need them for? She put a rolled tube of paper into the powder and sniffed hard, ooh! It felt good. Ann watched the men laughing and could see the other girls shrinking, thinking they could be next. The only interest the men had was to get this girl into the special room kept for very important dealings in the drug business and the door was sealed from the inside. The other girls were told to go to their rooms and await their masters there, they went away quickly, pleased to be gone. Leading the drugged girl by her arm they manoeuvred her into the business room. Closing the door with the seal they lifted her up onto the mahogany long table, stripping off their clothing and turning up the lights so they shone directly onto her. A camera rolled out from a cupboard and was switched on and one by one they took out their obscenities on the young girl. Although she was conscious it appeared she was enjoying doing all these horrendous things. Eventually she fell asleep or unconscious, only then did they stop and turn off the film making machine. Ann wished the police would hurry up, the yacht was heading out to sea and was picking up knots. The harbour police hadn't wasted any time and were already on their way in a speed boat with their passengers. The water was still choppy and the passengers were feeling it, the inspectors were not used to being off dry land and were clinging on for dear life. With lights and sirens flashing they pulled in close to the side of the yacht, which had slowed down and was waiting for them to board. As the steps were lowered, one by one the officers climbed aboard and the skipper queried them. "What is the reason you have for stopping our outgoing journey?" The inspector opened up his briefcase producing a summons and handed it to him. "You sir" He said. "Have to turn this yacht around as we have reason to believe there is contraband aboard". The skipper seemed to be alarmed, "Sir, believe me there is no item on this yacht that can be said to be contraband. We were cleared to leave the port and are already late, this delay will only upset the owner who will blame me for his loss of profit that he is expecting on the sale of this yacht". "I apologise for that sir" The inspector said "Now that you understand, you have five minutes to inform your owner of what is happening and turn the boat back to harbour". The skipper rang down to tell the owner about the situation and warn him they were about to search the whole yacht. The customs officers had arrived in another boat, climbed aboard and began searching the interiors. The men that previously were in the business room were now playing a friendly game of cards and drinking coffee, they looked all innocent and surprised when the officers walked in on them. "I have just been informed by my Captain". The owner of the yacht said. "That we have to turn around as you want to search my boat, what makes you believe we have anything to declare that is against the law of your land?" Standing up and turning to the others he said. "I think you all ought to go to your wives as these men are about to intrude into your quarters". He turned to the customs officers saying. "Other men must not attempt to mix with our females, this is not allowed in our religion". Ann was seeing and hearing all this, what could she do? The business room was well hidden and had become another wall, it would be found if the boat returned to harbour but not until then. The young girl was still laying unconscious inside and the other girls it seems were to mascaraed as the men's wives, they had covered their tracks. She moved back into the business room and she could see the girl was only this side of death and if she was going to live something had to be done soon as she was just hanging on to life. Ann leaned in to her and could feel her heart beating, if only spasmodically. "Don't die". Ann said. "If you want them to do this to others then go ahead and watch it happen as I am watching you". The girl opened her eyes. "Help me" She said. "Can you see me?" Ann asked. "Yes, will you help me?" Ann was astonished, being close to death had enabled the girl to break through the barrier. "You have to make a noise and let them know you are here, I don't know how you can do this but it's your last chance, so do something". The yacht rolled in the choppy waves and the mahogany table was shiny. The girl slid onto the floor with a bang. Ann realized the customs officers would have heard it and she hoped the young girl would survive, her eyes were closed now so she couldn't tell. She hadn't reached her side yet so there was still hope for her.

"What the hell was that"? The question was asked by one of the custom officers. "Came from over there". Another officer answered. "The seas are rough tonight". The yacht owner said, appearing agitated. Continuing with. "Something probably hasn't been fastened down, I will inform the captain and get this corrected before any damage is done". He went to leave the cabin and an officer blocked his way. "Sorry sir". He said. "If the skipper has heard it I am sure he will sort it out, but you know and we also know that the noise came from over there. What, I ask myself could be tucked away behind a wall, it is indeed a puzzle and very strange, could it be hidden contraband?" The owner dropped onto the couch saying. "If you believe I am hiding things then go ahead and find it, you are all being ridicules". He started coughing heavily, "I need some fresh air" He said between coughs. "May I go up to the deck"? "Give him a bloody drink of water and make sure he stays there until we find out what's behind that wall". The officer was losing his patience. Whilst they were looking for where the noise came from the owner of the boat went up onto the deck, accompanied by a female officer. He was still coughing and asked for his drink of water. "You left it below" She answered him. "I need a drink" he said, coughing and retching. The female officer became worried the man looked about to choke. "Stay there and don't move away, I will fetch you a drink". He nodded his reply and she went below, a few minutes passed before returning to the deck as she was intrigued by all the commotion that was happening there. The wall had been broken down and a girl was found naked, crouched into a ball. The female officer stood there staring for a second or two before hurrying back to the owner on deck. He wasn't where she had told him to be and it annoyed her. Moving around the upper deck she called out his name, no answer came. This was going to cause her a heap of trouble as she shouldn't have left him alone. Maybe he had decided to be with his friends in their cabins, it was very cold on deck. She would have to find him before the Inspector found out. The cabins lay on either side of a passageway, which was decorated beautifully. The officer knocked gently on the door of one cabin and a girl with her face covered, opened it. "I am looking for the owner of this boat, is he with you?" She asked. The girl shook her head and pointed to the opposite cabin. "Thank you" She said knocking on the other door. "Come in" A harsh voice answered. Turning the handle and opening the door she stepped inside, only to find herself looking into the barrel of a gun. It was unexpected but she needed to stay calm. "Put the gun away sir, this situation will not be remedied if you insist on stopping us doing our duty". "You can tell them to get off my boat or your life will be forfeit". He threw a phone at her. "They found a girl unconscious, could that be the reason you are pointing that at me?" He motioned her to pick up the phone, she did and rang the Inspector. "I am down in the cabins sir" She said. "What are you doing there? I told you to look after the owner upstairs". "I was sir" She answered. "Now I am in the cabin with him and he is holding a gun to my face and says if you don't get off his boat he will shoot me". The Inspector couldn't believe what he was hearing, the man had the audacity to hold one of his officers a prisoner. "I require you and you" He said pointing to two officers who were with the girl. "To get her aboard the Helicopter, it should be here shortly. We have another important thing to attend to". He stopped talking for an intake of breath and then continued. "In the cabins below stairs an officer has been held at gunpoint and is in grave danger, therefor we have to be very careful with our negotiations. The person holding the gun is the owner and by now knows the girl and the drugs have been found." He paused again, rubbing a hand over his chin. "I shall go first". He said." The four armed officers shall follow and if my persuasion doesn't work it will be up to you four to take him out, as we cannot afford to lose an officer". The phone rang again and the Inspector answered. "Yes, yes we are coming now". Turning and asking his four officers to follow him and to keep out of sight, he started down the stair and was soon outside of the cabins. He had no idea which cabin the officer was being held in, he rang his phone again and the sound came from the centre cabin. He switched it off and slowly opened the door. "Put your hands in the air". The owner waved the gun at him. "I have already tied your officer and you can put your hands behind you, and don't try anything or your woman will get it first". The Inspector needed to negotiate and it seemed this man wasn't going to. "May I first ask you what it is that you want us to do and maybe then I can arrange for my men to follow your requirements?" "What I want" The man said. "Is for you all to get off my boat and take that stupid girl with you. She stole drugs and brought them aboard my boat, and for this I cannot forgive her, she got herself in that state". The Inspector listened but he had heard clever liars before and this man was digging his own grave. It would have taken a dozen men to carry all that cocaine powder on board and stash it between the walls, she was to be admired if she could do all that on her own and not be noticed. "We understand sir" the inspector wanted to avoid being tied up. "The girl was an addict, which is no fault of yours. It is just a pity that we had to stop you leaving port. I suggest though sir that you untie my officer and we shall forget about the firearms. We shall wrap up our investigations taking the girl for further inquiries. I do believe the Helicopter is already overhead with her on the way to the hospital". The man gave a quick glance toward the porthole window and the Inspector jumped on him and at the same time shouting to the others outside, who rushed in. There was a shot fired and all went deathly quiet, had the men killed him? He was sprawled in a corner blasted by his own gun with half his brains blown out.

"That was a stupid thing you did to yourself, made a horrible mess too". Ann was standing beside him and he was looking down onto his body. "It really is you there, you bled to death". Ann laughed at him. "It serves you right, you have destroyed so many lives but this time you took your own". He was puzzled and not sure of what was happening. The policemen were in the room and there had been a shot he looked at himself and he was fine, perhaps one of them had got it. The bimbo was laughing at him, who the hell was she? "Why don't you take a good look at that body?" The girl was taunting him. He was dressed well he thought and his shoes were the same make as his. In fact he appeared very similar to himself except he was here and this man was dead. "Can you see the face? Have another look". Ann was enjoying this. He moved in closer to the body and seeing the brains spreading onto the floor sickened him. The face was like his, but he was feeling fine so it couldn't be him. "It is you" She shouted. "Look again, you are dead". Ann felt like shaking him. He reached his hand out to pick up the fallen gun, and he couldn't touch it. He wasn't going to stand there being laughed at by a woman, twice more he tried and the bitch was still laughing. "Are you completely stupid? You are not in their world now and you will have to answer for all your sins to a higher authority. Your journey is not yet over and I am pleased I am able to inform you, of what could be termed as paying a penance for past deeds". The man was starting to realize the body was his and felt the pain as they hoisted his remains into a black body bag. He was feeling unspeakable agony of broken bones being twisted and turned, and he knew hell was getting close. Ann would be there to help him on his last journey and happily say her goodbyes. The Inspector locked the cabin door, leaving an officer to guard it. The dead man's friends waited with the girls next door and this was where the Inspector was heading. The girls were huddled into a corner when he entered, and the men were standing together talking in their own language. "I have sad news for you all" The Inspector interrupted their conversation. "Your friend the owner of this yacht has had an accident, for which we are extremely sorry. Especially now as he will not have to serve a prison sentence". Once more their language filled the air and the eldest of the men stepped forward. "We heard the shot and we know you killed him we hold you responsible for his accident, if this is what you wish to call it". "This can be discussed later" The Inspector answered, he wasn't going to have these people tell him what he should call anything. "Meanwhile" He continued. "I wish to speak with your ladies, who if I may say so look extremely young for such elderly gentlemen". The Inspector walked over to the ladies in the corner and lifted one girls face with his hands, looking into her eyes. "Are you married to one of these gentlemen? He asked, and her eyes opened wide with fear. Turning to his officers he said. "Take them outside and arrest the gentlemen, and I say that loosely". The four men were cuffed and taken outside of the cabin and now the inspector hoped to get some answers. The female officer came in to assist him and sat beside them. "You will not be hurt if you tell the inspector who you are and where you come from". She said. "They are not your husbands, are they? She seemed to be getting through to them, as one after another said no. Needle marks on their arms told the Inspector what he wanted to know, regarding the drugs. The girls needed to feel safe before they would disclose what had been happening to them and at the moment they were unsure of the consequences if they spoke out. The men were taken into the hold under arrest and the girls stayed in the cabin as the boat sailed back to the shore. The customs officers were busy searching the interior and their findings were much more than they expected to find. Stashed behind the fittings in every cabin was large packets of Cocaine which would amount to multi thousands of pounds on the street and the money was to be used to buy arms from illicit dealers. These men were not only drug dealers, they were dealers in death and destruction of humanity even their own kind. The Inspector was well pleased with the results, of cause there would be others on the other side of the water who were waiting to collect the drugs. The inspector would never be able to arrest them but he had got their dealers and drugs, he felt satisfied with the results.

Back on shore, the boat owner's body was taken for an autopsy and the rest of his companions held under lock and key until they could all be questioned. The girls were taken to a hospital where they would be examined and if possible cleared of the drugs, before it was their time for questions. He himself was ready for a stiff drink but until he got back to the station with his reports the drink would have to wait. He rang the hospital, wanting to know how the injured girl was doing. "Still in a coma" The Doctor said. "She is as steady as we can expect her to be, considering the trauma she has been through. If or when there is any change we shall inform you immediately". "Thank you" The Inspector answered. "I am going back to my police station tonight and I can be contacted there, if there is anything you need please let my station know and thank you once again" Putting the phone down he wiped his brow with the back of his hand, he was feeling quite exhausted. His driver was waiting outside and his bag was packed, taking a lift down he left the building and was soon on his way. Closing his eyes, only for a moment he drifted off to a sleep. The driver could hear his snoring and smiled, he knew how tired the boss was so left him to sleep. An hour down the road and The Inspector awoke. "You should have put the sirens on and kept me awake, sorry but I didn't mean to fall asleep during the journey. It's just that I am completely knackered, another night of chasing boats and riding high in the waves is enough to make me want to leave the force. The sleep has calmed my nerves and I feel rejuvenated again". He shifted his position and sat upright looking out of the car window. "How long before we reach the station?" He asked his driver. "Not long now sir" came the answer. "Thirty minutes at the most". The driver too was tired, he had been waiting for some time for the Inspector to get back from his so called boat trip and he too needed a kip, this had been a long shift but almost over for now. The city lights shone out in the darkness and the car went into robot function, manoeuvring toward them.

Gerald and Ann's mother Vicky were strolling hand in hand in the stations garden and were becoming firm friends. Ann and her mother had lived on their own since Vicky's husband had left four years previously, he had run away with a woman ten years younger than himself. She was gently unfolding this tale to Gerald, who in return was very sympathetic. "Together" He said. "We could make beautiful music". Vicky had heard this before but coming from him a melody was beginning. Ann couldn't believe her mother was being so soppy, she had never seen her this way before. It was good to see her smiling again, maybe when all this horrible trouble is locked away in the archives her mother will have Gerald as a valuable friend to take care of her. Ann had needed to move away from the boat as she found her spirits sensitive side couldn't watch the torture being endured by the shot man. Although he was dead it didn't rule out his evil mind, the pain was living within his soul and would persist through all eternity. She too was dead but not suffering the way he was. If only she could tell her mother how much she loved and missed her. It was all her fault, why hadn't she listened? The girl in the coma had seen her before and had no idea she was lingering between life and death. If she came out of the coma she would be able to tell her mother how much she missed her and also that she was fine now. Ann's thoughts carried her through into the hospital, she looked down at the bed and at the girls pale face. "Are you awake?" she asked the girl. Her eyes stayed closed. Slowly an image of the girl arose above her bed and hovered there, she spoke to Ann. "I have seen you before". She seemed puzzled. "I don't understand what is happening, I am laid on the bed and at the same time I am here talking with you.

It is frightening me, can you please explain this? Ann was ready with an answer for her. "Don't be afraid" She said. "You have been very ill and right now you are in Limbo. I am sorry to say it is between life and death and that is why you can see me. The truth is you almost died and you are still not in a safe place, you have to keep on fighting". "Will you help me?" The girl asked Ann. "You have to push yourself back into your body". Ann answered. "It will be hard and you have to awaken your heart beat before it stops completely". The girl floated down to where her body lay, still looking puzzled. "When you do awaken, and I am sure you will". Ann said. "Would you give a message to my mother to say, I am well and happy and I will visit her in dreams. I wish her well and say, I love her with all my heart and please remember to say that I like her friend". The girl's image faded and Ann could see she was moving into her body and then the image was gone. She stayed there until the sound of bells began ringing, bringing doctors and nurses around the bed. Ann knew the girl was on her way back. The Inspector arrived at the station and his driver brought the luggage in, both of them were tuckered out and made for the nearest coffee machine. It wasn't the best it was strong and black and full of caffeine which they both needed. The Inspector had to report to the Chief before he could turn in and he was in for surprising news. The capture of the two foreign men at the airport had admitted, under intense questioning to procuring girls for sale. They would say who bought the girls if they would be lenient with their sentence. "We can't be lenient with them, can we?" The Inspector asked. "It's not for us to say" The Chief answered. "The judge will look at it closely and he alone will decide the outcome". All the gang were now under arrest and the girls are being looked after, the case was finally coming to a close and the courts would eventually seal it. It was a big relief for the Inspector and he went to tell Ann's mother. She was still in the gardens talking with Gerald when the Inspector walked toward her with a broad smile on his face." Excuse this interruption" He said. "There is something I have to tell you". Ann's mother, Vicky knew it had to be important and was puzzled as to what it could be. "We have arrested the whole gang and the two men from the airport have admitted to procuring girls for prostitution. It won't be long before they disclose the buyers of these girls and Interpol will do the rest". Gerald placed his arm around her, she was shaking and her tears flowed. "Thank you" she said to the Inspector. "I am so grateful for what you have done for my daughter and myself". Turning to Gerald she said. "I would like to go back inside now". With his arm still around her he walked her slowly into the station. Derek and Cindy wondered what had happened as Vicky was so distressed, Gerald found Vicky a seat and got her a cup of coffee before telling Derek and Cindy what it was all about. "I believe it was such a relief for Vicky to hear they are all under lock and key that it overwhelmed her and she couldn't hold the tears back. She will be fine after this". He said, sitting himself down beside her. Derek and Cindy chatted together and decided it was time to return to the church, they were hoping another contact could be made. Upstairs was where Derek had seen the spirit and they would have to go there as he needed to prepare his music for the evenings service. Making their excuses to Gerald and Vicky the two of them left the police station on their way to the church. Derek had grown very fond of Cindy and she was of him. It was as if they had been friends forever, an electric current made her tingle whenever he came close. The church had a musty smell and Cindy took a perfume bottle out of her pocket and sprayed it around. Derek asked her not to do it and she placed the bottle back into her pocket. She didn't ask why and Derek didn't offer any explanation but went up to the balcony and she followed him. After leaving the hospital Ann was hanging around in the church, it was a peaceful place and she felt enveloped in its love. She had an idea that her mother may return and she wanted to be present when she did. A scent drifted into her nostrils, it was horrid and it affected her senses. She realized someone had entered the church and whoever it was must have sprayed that obnoxious smell, she would have to remember scents and bleach upset her spirit. Up on the balcony the air was pure and Ann was waiting to see who was about to come up the stairs. She recognized Derek's voice which made her giggle, not that there was anything wrong with his voice. It was deep and strong making echoes ring in the walls around her. Noise in spirit affected her differently to when she was on the earth plane. Derek turned around, could he have heard her? She would have to be more careful she was not here to frighten anyone. Derek had seen her once before, he definitely wouldn't be frightened but there was someone behind him and they could get scared. It was her friend Cindy, how well and happy she was and it was easy to see Derek and she were in love. The two of them were kissing passionately and Ann felt it was time to disappear. She didn't feel jealous she could only be happy for them both, it was just a feeling of not having the experience of being in love. Now she feeling sorry for herself and she wasn't supposed to think that way. Derek was showing Cindy a music disc which he wanted to play for her, kissing him on the cheek she sat down to listen. The music was beautiful Ann could have listened all night. She had decided tonight was the last time her energy would allow her to materialize. Derek she felt was ready to see her again before she said her farewells, her time on earth was running out. The church was open and the pews were filling rapidly. Cindy went down into the church leaving Derek to play his music and while the sound filled the rafters Ann made her move. Derek pulled his jacket closer around him and rubbed his arms. "This place needs the heaters on" He said to himself. "It's so very cold". Then he realized the reason for the cold, Ann was standing before him, a radiant image. Her long hair floated over her face and she smiled and giggled to him. "Thank you and God bless you all". She said still smiling at Derek. Her words trailed off as she began to slowly fade. "Good bye". She said and was gone, this time for good. The music played on and with all those people in the church not a soul had noticed, excepting Ann's soul which was now at peace in eternity. "May she rest in the hands of Jesus". Derek said before joining in with the congregation at prayer. After service Derek told Cindy of the visitation and how she thanked everyone before saying good bye. "Is she really gone? "Cindy asked. "This time she said her final good bye". Derek answered. "And I felt honoured to be able to see her". Cindy squeezed his arm. "Come on". She said. "Tell me back at the hotel". "Ok" he replied and they headed back. The unconscious girl in the hospital had recovered enough to give the police all the evidence they needed and she had been speaking to Ann's mother by satellite. She told her everything Ann had said to her, as promised. "She loves you very much and said she will see you in your dreams, she also likes your friend". Ann's mother Vicky had a tear in her eye but a smile on her face, she thanked the young girl wishing her to get well soon and turned the set off.

It was a big court case and in the end the men got their well-earned sentences. It seemed they had prostitutes all over the City and other places too and mostly under the age of eighteen, younger than that were procured for foreign clients. Drug running and monies earned, belonged to the Cuban Mafia. Interpol knew of these gangs and arrested some when the chance arose but there were always others to take their place. The men the police had caught were expendable in the mafia's eyes and if they spoke out their families would die, so silence reined. This was a never ending challenge for the police who knew young people would continue dying because greedy gangs filled their own pockets with their money. Cindy settled into married life with Derek and at the last count had three children, two girls who were being taught to play the piano, the last one was too young he had only just arrived on the scene. Gerald and Vicky were on their honeymoon, it had taken a few years for Vicky to say yes to his proposal. She did love him but happiness she didn't think should be hers until one night in a dream Ann appeared to her saying. "You haven't lost me I will always be close, I cannot rest because you deny yourself happiness and for that I am sad. Your friend loves you and will take good care of you. Say yes you will marry him and I love you". When Vicky awoke the dream was still vivid, it was almost real and she consented to his proposal. Gerald was surprised and she never told him why she had succumbed and said yes. She didn't have any more children, maybe it wasn't to be or she was too afraid to try again. Gerald was fine, with or without children his life with Vicky was one big honeymoon.

Lightning Source UK Ltd.
Milton Keynes UK
UKOW04f2354221214

243583UK00001B/25/P